比较文学与世界文学 研究丛书

主编 曹顺庆

三编 第 **26** 册

李白望月的 150 种方式（下）

张 智 中 著

花木兰文化事业有限公司

国家图书馆出版品预行编目资料

李白望月的 150 种方式（下）／张智中 著 —— 初版 —— 新北市：
花木兰文化事业有限公司，2024〔民 113〕
目 10+264 面；19×26 公分
（比较文学与世界文学研究丛书 三编 第 26 册）
ISBN 978-626-344-825-4（精装）
1.CST：唐诗 2.CST：翻译
810.8   113009378

ISBN-978-626-344-825-4

9 786263 448254

比较文学与世界文学研究丛书
三编 第二六册   ISBN：978-626-344-825-4

李白望月的 150 种方式（下）

作　　者 张智中
主　　编 曹顺庆
企　　划 四川大学双一流学科暨比较文学研究基地
总 编 辑 杜洁祥
副总编辑 杨嘉乐
编辑主任 许郁翎
编　　辑 潘玟静、蔡正宣　美术编辑 陈逸婷
出　　版 花木兰文化事业有限公司
发 行 人 高小娟
联络地址 台湾 235 新北市中和区中安街七二号十三楼
　　　　　电话：02-2923-1455 ／传真：02-2923-1452
网　　址 http://www.huamulan.tw 信箱 service@huamulans.com
印　　刷 普罗文化出版广告事业
初　　版 2024 年 9 月
定　　价 三编 26 册（精装）新台币 70,000 元

李白望月的 150 种方式(下)

张智中 著

目

次

望月之 72：Midnight Moon: Lightness or Heaviness?（午夜之月：亦轻? 亦重? ）

读英文

They both went up to the **window**, and **through a slit in the shutter** they saw M. Bonacieux talking with a man in a cloak.

他们走到窗前，从窗户的一条缝隙中看到波那瑟先生正和一个身裹披风的人交谈。

She has an **ethereal** beauty.

她有一种微妙飘逸之美。

The love with which his young wife had inspired him was a secondary sentiment, and was not strong enough to contend with the primitive feelings we have just enumerated.

他对自己那位年轻妻子的爱情排在第二位，根本无法与我们上面说的他身上那些原始的本性相抗衡。

He was **momentarily** dazzled by the strong sunlight.

强烈的阳光使他一时睁不开眼。

Madame Bonacieux kissed the queen's hands, concealed the paper in the bosom of herdress, and disappeared with **the lightness of a bird**.

波那瑟夫人亲吻了王后的手，然后把信藏在怀里，鸟一般轻盈地消失了。

英文散译

Midnight Moon: Lightness or Heaviness?

The depth of night sees the moonlight whitening the window, and through a slit in the shutter, a beam steals into the room, straight across the ground while coating it with an ethereal film of rime. The nostalgia with which the moon has inspired me is so great that my heart, whose heaviness is momentarily relieved by the lightness of the moonlight, is heavy once again.

英文诗译

Midnight Moon: Lightness or Heaviness?

The depth of night sees the moonlight whitening the window,
and through a slit in the shutter,
a beam steals into the room,
straight across the ground while
coating it with an ethereal film
of rime. The nostalgia with
which the moon has inspired
me is so great that my heart,
whose heaviness is momentarily
relieved by the lightness of the
moonlight, is heavy once again.

回译

午夜之月：亦轻？亦重？
深夜，月光照白窗户；
从窗户的一条缝隙中，
一束光潜入卧室，
径直越过地面，并洒上
一层薄薄的、似有
若无的飘逸之霜。

月亮之轻盈，缓解

我心之痛。月亮

引发我的乡愁——

这乡愁啊，如此之重，

我的刚刚缓释的心，

再次，变得沉重……

译人语

译诗标题《午夜之月：亦轻？亦重？》（Midnight Moon: Lightness or Heaviness?），具散文之美。译诗前六行是一个句子：The depth of night sees the moonlight whitening the window, and through a slit in the shutter, a beam steals into the room, straight across the ground while coating it with an ethereal film of rime，回译："深夜，月光照白窗户；从窗户的一条缝隙中，一束光潜入卧室，径直越过地面，并洒上一层薄薄的，似有若无的飘逸之霜。"英文 The depth of night sees 这种无灵主语的优势，无法翻译出来；ethereal 也措词形象，汉语"似有若无的飘逸"，虽然繁琐，却大体对应其意。

译诗第二个句子：The nostalgia with which the moon has inspired me is so great that my heart, whose heaviness is momentarily relieved by the lightness of the moonlight, is heavy once again，回译："月亮之轻盈，缓解我心之痛。月亮又引发我的乡愁——这乡愁啊，如此之重，我的刚刚缓释的心，再次，变得沉重……"其中，"月亮之轻盈，缓解我心之痛"，英文靠后，中文前提。同时，中文回译的最后，采用省略号，英文却是句号。仔细想想，各有道理。反复读之，似乎还是英文更有味道，盖因发挥了英文长句之优势。

望月之 73：Moon-Provocative Heights of Emotion in the Height of Night（夜未央，情正浓——都是月亮惹的祸）

读英文

I wouldn't go there in the **height** of summer.
我不会在盛夏时节去那里的。

All was at peace in the dead of the night.
深夜里，万籁俱寂。

The power of music goes much, much further.
音乐的力量，影响更为深广。

It can **lift us out of depression** when nothing else can.
当没有办法之时，它可以帮助我们摆脱抑郁。

When he closed his eyes, he could **conjure up** in exact color almost every event of his life.
一闭上眼睛，他就能真真切切地回忆起他生命中几乎每一件事情。

Music can **move us to the heights or depths of emotion**.
音乐可以使我们达到情感的高度或深度。

英文散译

Moon-Provocative Heights of Emotion in the Height of Night

All is at peace in the dead of the night, and I can feel the power of the moon when I catch a glimpse of the floor silvery with seeming rime. The moment I lift my gaze toward the moon, I am lifted out of depression as the moon conjures up the fond memories of my innocent childhood in my native land — and I am moved to the heights of emotion.

英文诗译

Moon-Provocative Heights of Emotion in the Height of Night

All is at peace in the dead
of the night, and I can feel
the power of the moon when
I catch a glimpse of the floor
silvery with seeming rime.
The moment I lift my gaze
toward the moon, I am lifted
out of depression as the moon
conjures up the fond memories
of my innocent childhood in
my native land — and I am
moved to the heights of emotion.

回译

夜未央，情正浓——都是月亮惹的祸
深夜，万籁俱寂。
我感到月之力量——
当我看到银白色
的地面，似乎
着霜。抬头望月，
我便摆脱抑郁——
当月亮令我
回忆我的故乡，
那天真的童年

时代的美好回忆。
于是，我感动，我
激动—— 情难自禁。

译人语

英文诗题 *Moon-Provocative Heights of Emotion in the Height of Night*，两用 height，回译分别为"夜未央"与"情正浓"；Moon-Provocative，乃是造词："月亮惹的"之意。另外，译文中，all is at peace，the power of the moon，I am lifted out of depression，the moon conjures up the fond memories，I am moved to the heights of emotion 等，若不借鉴英文，一般译者，包括英美译者，很难译出这样生动的语言。

汉语回译中，"着霜"，乃地道汉语；"我感动，我激动——情难自禁"，与 I am moved to the heights of emotion 并非字面对应，却深层情感等值。有时，译文总难达到一眼看去的等值。例如 conjure up，大意为"想起；使在脑海中显现；用魔法召唤"，用在句子中：the moon conjures up the fond memories，非常形象，而汉语回译"当月亮令我回忆"，却平淡多了。

望月之 74：Romance of the Wakeful Moon（不眠之月的浪漫）

读英文

The children are **wakeful** tonight.

今晚小孩们还没入睡。

We **slid down** the grassy slope.

我们顺着草坡滑下去。

Music is **irresistible, haunting, and unforgettable**.

音乐难以抵挡、徘徊不去、难以忘记。

A single glance will tell you how hot or cold your tap water is with the Chameleon faucet.

只要安上一个"变色龙"牌水龙头，你就能一眼看出自来水的温度。

Out of an unexpected journey, Sacks has woven an unforgettable narrative which **immerses us in the romance of** island life, and shares his own compelling vision of the complexities of being human.

基于一次意想不到的旅行，萨克斯讲述了一个令人难忘的故事，我们听着，陶醉其中，想象着岛上的浪漫生活。同时，他还谈到复杂的人性，并分享了自己的独特观点。

Our **exquisite sensitivity to music** can sometimes go wrong.

我们对于音乐的精致的敏感度，有时也会出错。

英文散译

Romance of the Wakeful Moon

Splashes of moonlight? Or glittering of hoarfrost? When my wakeful gaze slides down to the strange floor before my strange bed, I seem to be in a trance. Moon gazing, in the dead of the night, is irresistible, haunting, unforgettable; a single glance of the moon immerses me in the romance of my remote childhood of my dim and distant hometown. Extraordinarily exquisite is my sensitivity to the moon, the familiar moon, particularly in this strange room of a strange land.

英文诗译

Romance of the Wakeful Moon

Splashes of moonlight?

Or glittering of hoarfrost?

When my wakeful gaze

slides down to the strange floor

before my strange bed, I seem

to be in a trance. Moon gazing,

in the dead of the night, is

irresistible, haunting, unforgettable;

a single glance of the moon

immerses me in the romance

of my remote childhood of

my dim and distant hometown.

Extraordinarily exquisite is my

sensitivity to the moon, the familiar

moon, particularly in this

strange room of a strange land.

回译

不眠之月的浪漫

月光闪烁？白霜

焕然？当我的不眠
之眼，滑向陌生
床下的陌生地面时，
我恍惚了。观月，
在这死寂的夜晚，
难以抵挡、徘徊
不去、难以忘记。
只消瞥上一眼，月亮
便使我陶醉其中，
令我回想着久违的
童年生活的浪漫——
在我遥远缥缈的故乡。
我有着非常精致的
敏感度——对于月亮，
对于这熟悉的月亮，
特别是在这陌生的土地上，
在这陌生的房间。

译人语

译诗标题 *Romance of the Wakeful Moon*，对应回译《不眠之月的浪漫》，显然超越了对《静夜思》的字面胶着。译诗开头: Splashes of moonlight? Or glittering of hoarfrost?（月光闪烁？白霜焕然？）心理活动，描写细腻，由原诗"疑是地上霜"之"疑"生出。

其后: a single glance of the moon immerses me in the romance of my remote childhood of my dim and distant hometown.（只消瞥上一眼，月亮便使我陶醉其中，令我回想着久违的童年生活的浪漫——在我遥远缥缈的故乡。）英文很是地道，回译若有所失。最后，译诗用两个 strange，来写"陌生的土地"和"陌生的房间"，并用 familiar 来写"熟悉的月亮"，产生对比和反差。整体观之，英文译诗 16 行，汉语回译 18 行，同样译笔自由，不太拘泥。

望月之 75：The Moon Shines as the Compass of My Life（夜月灿烂，人生之罗盘）

读英文

A shaft of moonlight fell on the lake.
一束月光照在湖面上。

He smiled **frostily** and deliberately turned away.
他冷冷地笑了笑，便故意转身走了。

The years have **silvered** her hair.
岁月已使她的青丝似雪。

Sacks explores how catchy tunes **can subject us to hours of mental replay**.
萨克斯研究朗朗上口的曲调，如何能够让我们在思想上回放几个小时。

My knowledge all came in **drips and drabs** after I got there.
一切都是来港后一点一滴逐渐认识的。

We had to rely on a **compass** and a lot of luck to get here.
要到达这儿，我们只得靠罗盘和很大的运气。

Soon she could see the silver sickle of **the waning moon** rising above the trees, and that served as her **compass** as she climbed up and down the rocky undulations of the forest.

不久，她就看到了一钩银色的弯月，正升起在树林之上。走在林中高低起伏的岩石路上，她把月亮当做自己的罗盘。

Peter breathed in deeply, savoring the beauty of the night, and relishing the thought of **happy years to be spent** in Fairacre.

彼得深深呼吸，品味着夜晚之美；想到即将在费雷克斯度过愉快的岁月，心里就美滋滋的。

英文散译

The Moon Shines as the Compass of My Life

A shaft of moonlight shoots, through the window, frostily into the room, to silver the floor before my bed, when my hair has been silvered by the frosty years. A single glance at the moon subjects me to hours of mental replay of the past, particularly of the drips and drabs of my childhood in my native land. For a wanderer like me, the moon always shines as the compass of my life, wherever it is spent.

英文诗译

The Moon Shines as the Compass of My Life

A shaft of moonlight shoots,
through the window, frostily
into the room, to silver
the floor before my bed,
when my hair has been
silvered by the frosty
years. A single glance
at the moon subjects me
to hours of mental replay
of the past, particularly
of the drips and drabs of
my childhood in my native
land. For a wanderer like
me, the moon always shines

as the compass of my

life, wherever it is spent.

回译

> 夜月灿烂，人生之罗盘
> 一束月光照射，
> 透窗，冷冷如霜，
> 进入卧室，给我
> 床前的地面镀银，
> 而我的头发，也被
> 如霜的岁月镀了银。
> 月亮——只消看一眼
> 月亮，即令我想起
> 我的故乡，想起遥远的
> 过往，童年生活的点点
> 滴滴，几个小时，
> 一直缠绵在我心头上。
> 客居他乡，故乡之月，
> 总亮。夜月灿烂，
> 人生之罗盘：无论
> 我在彼乡，此乡……

译人语

译诗中，用了 frostily 和 frosty，强调了原诗中"疑是地上霜"之"霜"；又用了两次 silver，均为动词，而 silver 与 frost 又存在着类似关系，从而进一步强调了《静夜思》之"霜"。此字极为重要，暗示着人生的风霜雨雪，与故乡的温暖，形成鲜明的对比。

另外，译诗用 compass（指南针；罗盘）来比喻月亮，突发奇想矣——却不失新颖独到之处：岁月沧桑之中，月亮，带来人生的慰藉；月亮，正是我们人生的罗盘。

再看英译与回译之间，英文自然地道，作为从英文译诗翻译过来的回译，也竭力摆脱翻译腔，采用地道汉语。为此，变通总是不可避免的。例如，"月亮——只消看一眼月亮"，是英文 A single glance at the moon 的诗化译文；"想起我的故乡，想起遥远的过往，童年生活的点点滴滴，几个小时，一直缠绵在我心头上"，源自英文 subjects me to hours of mental replay of the past, particularly of the drips and drabs of my childhood in my native land，不求字面对应，但求情感等同。接下来，英文单词 wanderer，也没有翻译成"流浪者、漫游者"之类，用"客居他乡"，保证了措语不至于偏狭，而中文读者也容易产生情感共鸣。随后，"故乡之月，总亮。夜月灿烂，人生之罗盘：无论我在彼乡，此乡……"，再看英文：the moon always shines as the compass of my life, wherever it is spent，可见汉语之华丽与英文之平淡。均为各自语言之本色。

望月之 76：Midnight Moonlight Pregnant with Homesickness （月之光华，满含乡愁）

读英文

A silence fell on the two men.

两个人都沉默了下来。

Tom looked **in the direction that** the stranger pointed, and beheld one of the great trees.

汤姆朝陌生人指的方向望去，看到一棵大树。

All night long he sings, and **the cold, crystal moon looks down**, and the yew-tree spreads out its giant arms over the sleepers.

它整夜不停地唱着，水晶般的冷月俯望着大地，紫杉树张开巨大的手臂罩着在那里长眠的人。

As she did so, the moon came out from behind a cloud, and **flooded with its silent silver the little churchyard**, and from a distant copse a nightingale began to sing.

当她完成这一动作后，月亮就从云后出来了，给宁静的小墓园洒满了一片银光，远处的矮树丛里夜莺唱起了歌。

She **was rapt in thought** all evening.

她整晚上都陷入深深的沉思。

Nevertheless, it was an **eloquent** shrug, **pregnant with** prophecy.
然而，他这次耸肩却是意味深长，预示着什么事情。

英文散译

Midnight Moonlight Pregnant with Homesickness

A silence and frost fall on my bedside floor, as a beam of light steals, glittering through the window, into the room. Then I look in the direction that the beam shines, to find the cold, crystal moon looking down, flooding with its silent silver the little room, and I am rapt in thought all night. From the moon, it is an eloquent beam of moonlight, pregnant with homesickness.

英文诗译

Midnight Moonlight Pregnant with Homesickness

A silence and frost fall on my bedside floor, as a beam of light
steals, glittering through the
window, into the room. Then I
look in the direction that the beam
shines, to find the cold, crystal
moon looking down, flooding
with its silent silver the little
room, and I am rapt in thought
all night. From the moon, it is
an eloquent beam of moonlight,
pregnant with homesickness.

回译

月之光华，满含乡愁
寂静与白霜落在床前
的地上，而一束光，
轻轻悄悄，闪闪烁烁，
穿过窗户，进入卧室。

我朝着光亮的地方
望去，发现水晶般的
冷月俯照着大地，
给宁静的小小卧室
注满一片银光——我
整个晚上都陷入深深
的沉思。月之光华，
意味深长，满含乡愁。

译人语

译诗开头：A silence and frost fall on my bedside floor（寂静与白霜落在床前的地上），将抽象的 silence 和具象的 frost 并置，作为主语，句子便有了诗意。"水晶般的冷月"（the cold, crystal moon），没见过这样新颖的比喻，这里从英文句子中学来。译诗最后一个句子很好：From the moon, it is an eloquent beam of moonlight, pregnant with homesickness，初学英文者应该不容易理解。再看所借鉴的英文句子：Nevertheless, it was an eloquent shrug, pregnant with prophecy（然而，他这次耸肩却是意味深长，预示着什么事情）。其中，两个单词值得反复玩味：eloquent（雄辩的；有口才的；动人的）和 pregnant（怀孕的；充满的；意味深长的）。此句回译："月之光华，意味深长，满含乡愁。"翻译手法跳脱，同时又吻合译诗之标题：《月之光华，满含乡愁》，起到了扑题之作用。

望月之 77：A Moonlit Night, a Homesick Night（月照之夜，乡思之夜）

读英文

A snow year, a rich year.
瑞雪兆丰年。

Every time I close the door on reality, **it comes in through the window**.
我每次闭门不纳现实，它都从窗口进来。

The table **was coated in dust**.
桌子上覆盖了一层灰尘。

Good temper is like a sunny day; **it sheds its brightness everywhere**.
好情绪犹如明媚的阳光，普照四方。

Still waters run deep.
静水流深。

A man, a horse, and a dog **are never weary of each other's company**.
人、马、狗，可以永远相伴不厌倦。

英文散译

A Moonlit Night, a Homesick Night

Through the window moonlight comes in, falling aground, coating the floor before my bed in an ethereal film of frost. Upward glancing: the moon is shedding its brightness everywhere, when still night runs deep. The moon and me, we are never weary of each other's company. A moonlit night, a homesick night.

英文诗译

A Moonlit Night, a Homesick Night
Through the window moon-
light comes in, falling aground,
coating the floor before
my bed in an ethereal film
of frost. Upward glancing:
the moon is shedding
its brightness everywhere,
when still night runs deep.
The moon and me, we
are never weary of each
other's company. A moonlit
night, a homesick night.

回译

月照之夜，乡思之夜
月光从窗户
进来，落在
地上，把我
床前的地面，
镀上了一层
缥缈袅娜之霜。
抬眼望：月光
普照四方，静夜，
流深。我与月亮，
我俩永远相伴，
不厌倦。月照
之夜，乡思之夜。

译人语

　　模仿英文句子：A snow year, a rich year.（瑞雪兆丰年），便有了译诗之标题：*A Moonlit Night, a Homesick Night*（《月照之夜，乡思之夜》）。译诗中的英文单词 ethereal，词典解释为"天上的；飘逸的；精致的；飘渺的"，汉语回译为"缥缈袅娜"，似乎正好。因为成语 Still waters run deep（静水流深），译诗中的句子 still night runs deep，也具有了名言的性质。

　　"我与月亮，我俩永远相伴，不厌倦"（The moon and me, we are never weary of each other's company），把月光拟人化了，令人想起李白的《独坐敬亭山》中的名句："相看两不厌，只有敬亭山。"多年来，客居异乡，人事风物，何其沧桑巨变，唯有头顶一轮明月，不改其老旧之光，如皎如洁，多情照我。译诗结语："月照之夜，乡思之夜"（A moonlit night, a homesick night），重复译诗之标题。试图译出名句的效果，当为译者之追求。

望月之 78：Homesickness Nourished by Midnight Moon（乡愁油然，夜月朗）

读英文

A bird **is known by its note**, and a man by his talk.
闻声知鸣鸟，闻言见人心。

It was an abyss of green beauty and shady depths, pierced by vagrant **shafts of the sun** and mottled here and there by the sun's broader blazes.
这是一个深渊，里面绿叶茂密，阴凉处深不可测，但却被太阳游移不定的光线划破了，如火焰一般的太阳光把四处照得斑驳陆离。

Happiness often **sneaks in through a door** you didn't know you left open.
快乐往往从你忘记关好的门溜进来。

The bookshelves **were coated with** red paint.
书架上涂了一层红色的油漆。

Waddington **looked** at her **reflectively**. **Her abstracted gaze rested on** the smoothness of the river.
沃丁顿若有所思地望着她。只见她那漫不经心的目光落到了平静的河面上。

Desires **are nourished by** delays.
欲望迟迟得不到满足，会愈来愈强烈。

英文散译

Homesickness Nourished by Midnight Moon

The moon is known by its shafts of light, which sneak in through the window, and drop down, coating the bed-side floor with silvery rime. I look up reflectively into the high sky without the window, my abstracted gaze resting on the moon, by which my homesickness is nourished.

英文诗译

Homesickness Nourished by Midnight Moon

The moon is known
by its shafts of light,
which sneak in through
the window, and drop
down, coating the bed-
side floor with silvery
rime. I look up reflectively
into the high sky without
the window, my abstracted
gaze resting on the moon,
by which my home-
sickness is nourished.

回译

乡愁油然，夜月朗
深夜见光，
而知月——
悄然，潜入窗，
落我床前地面，
镀银，如霜。
若有所思，
抬眼望，窗外

高空清且爽——
漫不经心
之目光，落在
月亮上：乡愁
油然，夜月朗。

译人语

译诗标题 *Homesickness Nourished by Midnight Moon*，采用动词 nourish，出人意表，耐人寻味。回译:《乡愁油然，夜月朗》，nourish 微妙含义之美，只能舍弃，无可奈何。译文结尾: the moon, by which my homesickness is nourished（乡愁油然，夜月朗），重复了诗歌标题——英文是部分重复，中文则完全重复，从而带来回味的余地。中文回译中，音韵效果比较明显:"光，窗，霜，望，爽，光，上，朗"，一韵流注；汉字组合，从三个到四个、五个、六个、七个，参差错落，具宋词之风味矣。

望月之 79：As the Moon, So the Homesickness（明月千里，寄乡思）

读英文

As the call, **so the** echo.
发什么声音，有什么回声。

As the tree, **so the** fruit.
什么树结什么果。

The novelty of such change may even be **a source of** pleasure.
变化带来的新鲜感，或许还会成为乐趣的来源。

A good conscience **is a continual feast**.
问心无愧天天乐。

Day by day, after the December snows were over, a blazing blue **sky poured down torrents of light and air on the white landscape**, which gave them back in an intenser glitter.
十二月的雪季过了之后，一天又一天，蔚蓝的晴空向地面倾泻光明和空气，雪白的地面又更强更烈地把它们送回。

The news was **disheartening** for investors.
这条消息对投资者来说是令人灰心的。

Clyde wanted to say some **comforting** and **heartening** words to his mother.
克莱德要向母亲说一些安慰鼓励的话。

英文散译

As the Moon, So the Homesickness

The bedside floor is frosty with a beam of moonlight, whose source is traced without the window to the moon which is a continual feast, when the sky is pouring down torrents of light and air on the boundless white landscape. Disheartening is the deep night; comforting is the moonlight. As the moon, so the homesickness.

英文诗译

As the Moon, So the Homesickness
The bedside floor is frosty
with a beam of moonlight,
whose source is traced
without the window to the
moon which is a continual
feast, when the sky is pouring
down torrents of light and air
on the boundless white landscape. Disheartening is the
deep night; comforting is
the moonlight. As the moon,
so the homesickness.

回译

明月千里，寄乡思
床前的地面上，
月光照之，成霜。
其源：窗外冰壶，
月盈光满，精神
之飨——天空
向广袤的银白色
地面，倾泻着

光明和空气。
深夜，令人
沮丧；月光，
给人慰藉。明月
千里，寄乡思。

译人语

译诗诗题 *As the Moon, So the Homesickness*，仿写自前两个英文句子中的 as the … so the…结构，具有习语名言之性质；汉语回译《明月千里，寄乡思》则源自名言"明月千里寄相思"，加了个逗号，并改"相思"为"乡思"。从句 whose source is traced without the window to the moon which is a continual feast，回译："其源：窗外冰壶，月盈光满，精神之飨"，这里，用"冰壶"指代月亮，以避免与紧随其后的"月"字的重复，而且"月盈光满"，在汉语里，也属新鲜造语。Disheartening is the deep night; comforting is the moonlight.（深夜，令人沮丧；月光，给人慰藉。）句短而对比明显，令人读之而印象深刻。译诗结尾重复诗题：As the moon, so the homesickness.（明月千里，寄乡思。）夜既有月，而内心乡思。

望月之 80：A Still Moonlit Night & a Homesick Heart（静夜深，情缠绵）

读英文

Far down the street **he caught a glimpse of something that moved**.
沿街看去，他瞥见远处有什么东西在动。

The tide was going out, and the sand was smooth and **glittering**.
潮水正在退去，沙滩平坦，闪闪发亮。

I felt that my presence must be **a source of embarrassment to my friend**.
我觉得，我在他家的存在，一定是使我朋友感到为难的根源。

Politeness **costs nothing and gains everything**.
礼貌不用花一分钱，却能赢得一切。

A still tongue makes a wise head.
沉默者有智慧。

英文散译

A Still Moonlit Night & a Homesick Heart

I catch a glimpse of something that is glittering like frost on the floor before my bed, and slowly I trace the source of luminosity with my eyes to the moon in the silent night sky. The moonlight costs nothing and gains everything; a still moonlit night makes a homesick heart.

英文诗译

A Still Moonlit Night & a Homesick Heart
I catch a glimpse of
something that is glittering
like frost on the floor
before my bed, and
slowly I trace the source
of luminosity with my
eyes to the moon in the
silent night sky. The
moonlight costs nothing
and gains everything;
a still moonlit night
makes a homesick heart.

回译

静夜深，情缠绵
我睁眼，瞥见
闪光如霜的
东西，在我的
床前。慢慢地，
我移动目光，
寻光求源——
宁静的夜空
中，月亮正
圆。月光，
无所不能，
却无需花钱。
静夜深，情缠绵。

译人语

译诗标题 *A Still Moonlit Night & a Homesick Heart*，改写自译诗的最后两

行：a still moonlit night makes a homesick heart，只是去掉动词 make，并加上表示紧密并列的符号&，这样正好。汉语回译：《静夜深，情缠绵》，变通较大，以使其吻合诗题之语言特色。另一处回译："寻光求源"，乃是"寻求光源"的交叉搭配；如此，则造语鲜活，令人耐读。英文句子 The moonlight costs nothing and gains everything，非常经典，几成名言；而其回译："月光，无所不能，却无需花钱。"若有所失矣。另外，a still moonlit night makes a homesick heart，其中的 homesick，名言"乡愁、乡思"，而其回译"静夜深，情缠绵"，却变成普遍的情感，不见得一定是"思故乡"。翻译，总有所失。因此，译者总是寻求最佳的译语表达方式，失于此，补于彼，力求整体上的等值。月盈，心满。如此翻译《静夜思》，译笔才不会走偏。

望月之 81：The Moon & Homesickness（月寄乡思）

读英文

A burst of sunshine sent **a beam of amber light** through the window.
一道阳光透过窗户射进了一束琥珀色的光。

Chris lay on his back, his head propped by the bare jutting wall of stone, **his gaze** attentively **directed** across the canyon **to** the opposing tree-covered slope.
克里斯躺着，他的头枕在突出来的光秃秃的石头上，他的目光越过山谷，聚精会神地望着山谷对面长满树的山坡。

A holiday gives one a chance to look backward and forward, to **reset oneself by an inner compass**.
假期使你有机会回顾与前瞻，用心中的罗盘重新定好自己的方位。

She discovered it **in the midst of** sorting out her father's things.
她在整理父亲的东西时发现了它。

Beauty and folly are often companies.
漂亮与愚蠢常为伴侣。

英文散译

The Moon & Homesickness

The floor before my bed is silvery with a film of frost, whose luminosity is traced to a beam of light through the lattice window. I direct my gaze to the bright moon, my inner compass, by which to reset myself in the midst of daily pressures and perplexities, when the moon and homesickness are companies.

英文诗译

The Moon & Homesickness
The floor before my bed
is silvery with a film
of frost, whose luminosity
is traced to a beam of light
through the lattice window.
I direct my gaze to the bright
moon, my inner compass,
by which to reset myself
in the midst of daily
pressures and perplexities,
when the moon and home-
sickness are companies.

回译

月寄乡思
床前的地面，
着一层白霜
似的银光；探
其源：一束亮光，
正穿越花格之窗。
我抬眼，望着
月亮，我心中
的罗盘，重新
定好自己的方向
——面对日常的

压力与困惑——

当月亮与乡愁为伴。

译人语

英文译诗标题 *The Moon & Homesickness*，回译若为《月亮与乡愁》，淡而无味；现译为《月寄乡思》，诗意陡增。译诗前五行，与之前的译文，多有重复之处。变化却在后面七行，其实由一个句子构成：I direct my gaze to the bright moon, my inner compass, by which to reset myself in the midst of daily pressures and perplexities, when the moon and homesickness arc companies.（我抬眼，望着月亮，我心中的罗盘，重新定好自己的方向——面对日常的压力与困惑——当月亮与乡愁为伴。）使用了一个同位语和两个从句，非常符合英文长句之特色。

望月之 82: The Mid-Heaven Moon, a Home Returnee（半空之月照归人）

读英文

Both air and light, therefore, **penetrated in some measure into** the glade.
因此，空气和光线多多少少地渗入到这片空地上来。

The rooms were lofty, **a ripple of sunshine flowed** over the ceilings.
房间很高，一道闪烁不定的阳光在天花板上移动。

Occasionally **the effect of the moonlight on the waters was as though** the boat sailed across **a glittering silver field**. Little wavelets rippled along the banks. It was enchanting.
偶尔，月光照在水面上，船就像行驶在一片银光闪闪的水域上。微波沿着河岸泛开涟漪。这太迷人了。

The night continued clear. The moon, riding in mid-heaven, diffused her rays on all sides.
夜色依然明亮。半空中的月亮将光芒洒向四面八方。

Simon **fell into a reverie**, from which he was aroused by his wife.
西蒙陷入了沉思，他的妻子将他从沉思中唤醒。

But while Harry **was thus giving the rein to his imagination**, Jack Ryan, quitting the platform, had leaped on the step of the moving machinery.
但是正当哈里发挥他的想象力时，杰克·瑞安已经离开了平台，跳到了运转机器的阶梯上。

I fancied myself now like one of the ancient giants who were said to live in caves and holes in the rocks, where none could come at them.

现在，我觉得自己就像一个古代的巨人，据说他们就住在山洞或岩石上的洞穴里，在那里，没有人能伤到他们。

Decidedly, Athos, you were born to be a general, and the cardinal, **who fancies himself a great soldier**, is nothing beside you.

的确，阿托斯，你生来就是个将才，至于红衣主教，他总觉得自己是个伟大的军人，与你相比一文不值。

英文散译

The Mid-Heaven Moon, a Home Returnee

As a glittering beam of light penetrates in some measure into the little room, a ripple of moonshine is flowing over the bedside floor. The effect of the moonlight is as though the floor is frosty: a glittering silver ground. The night continues clear, and the moon, riding in mid-heaven, diffuses her rays on all sides. At this sight I fall into a reverie, and I am giving the rein to my imagination — I fancy myself now a home returnee ....

英文诗译

The Mid-Heaven Moon, a Home Returnee

As a glittering beam of light penetrates
in some measure into the little room,
a ripple of moonshine is flowing
over the bedside floor. The effect
of the moonlight is as though the floor
is frosty: a glittering silver ground.
The night continues clear, and the moon,
riding in mid-heaven, diffuses her rays
on all sides. At this sight I fall into
a reverie, and I am giving the rein

to my imagination — I fancy

myself now a home returnee ....

回译

半空之月照归人

一束亮光，或多或少地，

渗入小小的卧室；一道

闪烁不定的月光，在床前

的地面上忽闪，忽闪着。

月照屋内，地板似乎着霜：

一片银光多闪烁。夜色

依然明亮——半空中的

月亮，光洒四方。此情

可待成追忆：我陷入

沉思，开始遐想——

倏忽之间，我觉得自己

是个赶路人，正在归乡……

译人语

英文诗题 *The Mid-Heaven Moon, a Home Returnee*，若直译，则是："中天之月，归乡之人"，乃名词并列。回译《半空之月照归人》，有七言古诗之色调。译诗中，英文 is flowing over，回译"忽闪，忽闪着"，"忽闪"一词，本来形象，此处复用，以烘托月光如水闪闪烁烁之貌，效果较好。The effect of the moonlight，不可译为"月光之效果"；回译如何？却不见 effect 之痕迹——其实，effect 在英文中，既巧且妙，中文难以企及。只可意会而不可言传之词，当为妙语隽词。随后，英文 At this sight，简单朴实；回译"此情可待成追忆"，借李商隐名句来点缀，比原文更雅。刚才 effect 的回译，显然不及英文；这里的回译，当视为超越英文。翻译中，彼失此补，乃是常态。同样，I fall into a reverie，回译"我陷入沉思，开始遐想"，以及译诗最后的 I fancy myself now a home returnee ....，回译"我觉得自己是个赶路人，正在归乡……"，均为一语而双译，可谓深化之译。

从英文借鉴的角度来看，英译虽然不太繁琐，却大量借鉴英文，几乎无一字无来历。巧妙衔接、精心融合之后，通篇译文顺畅熨贴。整首译诗由四个句子组成，有从句，有插入，长短结合，舒缓相间；就标点符号而言，逗号句号之外，尚有省略号与破折号——从而有助于情感之抒发与宣泄。

望月之 83：Longing for Home in the Depth of Night（静夜，思乡）

读英文

I slept unquietly, dreamed always frightful dreams, and often **started out of my sleep in the night**.

晚上睡不安稳，老做恶梦，还常常从梦中惊醒。

A fireplace **lends coziness and cheer to** a room.

壁炉给房间带来温暖舒适和欢快气氛。

Gus **threw a moody glance skyward**.

格斯闷闷不乐地朝天空瞥了一眼。

He took a **detached** attitude to the matter.

他对那件事持超然的态度。

He is filled with a wild ecstatic happiness.

他欣喜若狂。

I **have a great longing for home**.

我非常想家。

On reaching his room he **entirely broke down**, and **became a prey to** the most violent agitation.

一回到自己的房间，他整个人就瘫倒了下来，并陷入了极度的焦虑之中。

英文散译

Longing for Home in the Depth of Night

All of a sudden I start out of my sleep in the depth of night, by a beam of silvery light, light of the moon, which lends a frosty film to the floor before my bed, as I throw a moody glance skyward: the moon hangs detachedly in the high sky. And I, filled with a great longing for home, entirely break down, and become a prey to a touch of nostalgia.

英文诗译

Longing for Home in the Depth of Night

All of a sudden I start out
of my sleep in the depth of
night, by a beam of silvery
light, light of the moon,
which lends a frosty film to
the floor before my bed, as I
throw a moody glance skyward:
the moon hangs detachedly
in the high sky. And I, filled
with a great longing for home,
entirely break down, and become
a prey to a touch of nostalgia.

回译

静夜，思乡
静夜，突然，
一束银光——
月亮之光，
把我从梦中
惊醒，给我床前
的地面，镀上

一层白霜。
情绪不佳，
我朝天望——
月亮超然悬高空。
想家思家更念家，
情不自禁乡愁生。

译人语

英文诗题 *Longing for Home in the Depth of Night*，回译《静夜，思乡》，有了逗号，便有了文气。译诗中，动词 start，"突然一惊"之意；light of the moon，作 a beam of silvery light 的同位语，补充说明。英译中，头韵明显，例如：sudden，start，sleep，silvery；I，night，by，light，my，skyward，high，sky，entirely；frosty，film，floor，before，filled，for 等，几组明显的头韵组合。另外，英文多地道之语言，如 become a prey to a touch of nostalgia，回译"情不自禁乡愁生"，只传其意。不过，汉语回译中，添加使用了两个破折号，表示时间的延长，亦具效果。

望月之 84：Homesickness Is Annexed to the Moon（乡愁系月）

读英文

Happiness **is not always annexed to** wealth.

幸福并不一定是财富的附属物。

His behavior was **suggestive** of a cultured man.

他的举止暗示他是一个有教养的人。

In a little while every sound ceased but his own voice; **every eye fixed itself upon him**.

不一会儿，除了他在讲话，所有声音都停止下来，每只眼睛都注视着他。

She **was pining for** her mother.

她思念着母亲。

The world **is his who** enjoys it.

活着感到快乐，世界就属于你。

英文散译

Homesickness Is Annexed to the Moon

A silvery film of frost on the floor before my bed is suggestive of a bright moon, upon which my eyes fix themselves after I glance up, and I begin to pine for my home. Homesickness is always annexed to the moon, and the moon is his who watches it.

英文诗译

Homesickness Is Annexed to the Moon

A silvery film of frost
on the floor before
my bed is suggestive
of a bright moon,
upon which my eyes
fix themselves after
I glance up, and I
begin to pine for my
home. Homesickness
is always annexed to
the moon, and the moon
is his who watches it.

回译

乡愁系月
床前地面
上，一层淡
淡的银霜，
令人想到
月光——
抬头望，我
的眼睛盯着
月亮：我便
开始思乡。
乡愁系月
——观月者，
月在心上。

译人语

　　第一个英文例子，Happiness is not always annexed to wealth，英文表达很

好，汉语译文："幸福并不一定是财富的附属物。"措词有些牵强。英译汉时，凡出现汉语牵强别扭之处，一般都是英文漂亮之时。译诗标题：*Homesickness Is Annexed to the Moon*，改造而出，不同凡响。再回译汉语：《乡愁系月》，大体可行。

整体看来，英文译诗由两个句子组成，长短结合，布局有致。英文虽然只用了逗号和句号，汉语回译却增译了两者之外的破折号与冒号。英文靓句在译诗最后：Homesickness is always annexed to the moon, and the moon is his who watches it，对应之回译："乡愁系月——观月者，月在心上。"同样具有名句效果。

望月之 85：The Moon: as Long as Homesickness（月亮长，乡愁亦长）

读英文

Art is long, life is short.
人生短暂，艺术长存。

The garden **is bright with** flowers.
鲜花满园。

He would **steal upward glances at** the clock.
他不时偷偷往上看钟。

Just at this crisis, as though she comprehended all this agitation regarding herself, **the moon shone forth with serene splendor**, eclipsing by her intense illumination all the surrounding lights.

恰恰在这个时候，月亮好像知道这阵骚动跟自己有关似的，发出宁静的光芒，周围所有的灯光都淹没在它明亮的光辉中。

Our mightiest feelings are always those which remain most unspoken.
最强烈的，总是那些缄默的感情。

英文散译

The Moon: as Long as Homesickness

My bedside floor is bright with a thin film of silvery frost, or moonlight?

Upward glancing to find the moon shining forth with serene splendor, I am reduced to homesickness: our mightiest feelings are always those which are connected to the moon. The moon is long, as long as homesickness.

英文诗译

The Moon: as Long as Homesickness

My bedside floor is bright
with a thin film of silvery
frost, or moonlight?
Upward glancing to find
the moon shining forth
with serene splendor, I am
reduced to homesickness:
our mightiest feelings are
always those which are
connected to the moon.
The moon is long, as
long as homesickness.

回译

月亮长，乡愁亦长
床前的地面——
明亮，因为
一层薄薄的
银霜？或者
月光？抬眼望，
只见月亮发出
宁静之光，
乡愁，便袭到我
心头之上。
最强烈的情感，

总是离不开月亮。

月亮长，乡愁亦长。

译人语

　　译诗标题 *The Moon: as Long as Homesickness*，其中的形容词 long，似乎不太好理解。读英文句子 Art is long, life is short（人生短暂，艺术长存），可知这里的 long，并非指物理概念的长度，而是时间概念的"长久"之意。那么，英文标题便是"月亮长久，乡愁亦长久"之意，简化后，回译为《月亮长，乡愁亦长》，更具诗意。

　　译文中，a thin film of silvery frost, or moonlight?（一层薄薄的银霜？或者月光？）生动地译出了"疑是地上霜"之心理状况。Our mightiest feelings are always those which are connected to the moon. The moon is long, as long as homesickness. 回译："最强烈的情感，总是离不开月亮。月亮长，乡愁亦长。"这两句，似乎译出了《静夜思》之灵魂。

望月之 86：The Moon: the Maze of Thought for Home（月亮：思乡之迷宫）

读英文

Spectators see clearly while the participants **are often lost in the maze**.

旁观者清，当局者迷。

A metallic ray of light flashed out from the summit of Half Dome, then a second and a third.

一束金属色的光线从半圆顶山的山顶上射出来，紧接着是第二束和第三束。

The mist **penetrated into** the room.

雾气渗进了室内。

All eyes were directed toward the person who spoke.

所有目光都投向了这个说话的人。

He watched with untiring patience the passage of the projectile across her **silvery disc,** and really the worthy man remained in perpetual communication with his three friends, whom he did not despair of seeing again some day.

凭借着不知疲倦的耐心，他日夜望着炮弹绕着银色月盘飞行。他真是一个可敬的人，一直以这种方式和他的朋友们保持着交流，并且希望能在未来的某一天重新看到他们。

The heads of both boys **were craned backward** on the instant, **agog with**

excitement.

两个男孩的头立即向后伸着脖子，兴奋不已。

英文散译

The Moon: the Maze of Thought for Home

The window is bright with a ray of light which flashes out from the night sky, before penetrating into the room to drop aground, making a frosty floor. When my eyes are directed toward the silvery disc, I am agog with excitement, and my head is craned backward, lost in the maze of thought for home.

英文诗译

The Moon: the Maze of Thought for Home

The window is bright

with a ray of light which

flashes out from the night

sky, before penetrating

into the room to drop

aground, making a frosty

floor. When my eyes are

directed toward the silvery

disc, I am agog with excite-

ment, and my head is craned

backward, lost in the maze

of thought for home.

回译

月亮：思乡之迷宫

窗户被一束光

照亮——闪烁

自夜空，然后，

穿窗入室，

落在地上，

铺洒地面如霜。
目光投向银色
月盘，我欣喜
不已：仰头
朝天，我迷失
在思乡的
迷宫之中。

译人语

英文译诗题目：*The Moon: the Maze of Thought for Home*（《月亮：思乡之迷宫》），呼应译诗的结尾：the maze of thought for home。是的，月亮，令人如此着迷，望之而不能自拔，思乡而不能自已——月亮，正是思乡的迷宫了，这是贴切而巧妙的比喻。

译文中，用 the silvery disc（银色月盘）来指月，不能理解。接下来，I am agog with excitement，其中，形容词 agog，意为"兴奋的；有强烈兴趣的"；and my head is craned backward，动词 crane，原为"起吊"之意，此处作"伸长（脖子）"之解。

望月之 87： An Ounce of Moonlight, a Pound of Gold（一盎司月光，一磅黄金）

读英文

An ounce of prudence is worth a pound of gold.
一盎司谨慎抵得上一磅黄金。

When that person arrived, Johnny was sleeping gently, and **gently he awoke** and allowed his pulse to be taken.
医生来的时候，他睡得很安稳。他慢慢地醒过来，让医生给他把脉。

"Where?" she finally asked, removing the apron from her head and **gazing up at him with a stricken face in which there was little curiosity.**
她拉下脸上的围裙，愁苦却几乎毫不惊奇地抬头盯着他，最后她问道："你要去哪里？"

She was **stricken** in years when I met her.
我见她时，她已年老体衰。

As he spoke, the tree across the street appeared with dazzling brightness **on his inner vision.**
他一面说着，一面觉得街对面的那棵树在他的心里似乎放出了耀眼的光。

英文散译

An Ounce of Moonlight, a Pound of Gold
The moon is shining brightly and gently into my room, when gently I awake from a fond dream, to find my bedside floor dreamily frosty. I gaze up at the moon

with a stricken face in which there is much sentimentality, and my native land seems to appear on my inner vision. An ounce of moonlight is worth a pound of gold.

英文诗译

An Ounce of Moonlight, a Pound of Gold

The moon is shining brightly

and gently into my room,

when gently I awake from

a fond dream, to find my

bedside floor dreamily frosty.

I gaze up at the moon with

a stricken face in which there

Is much sentimentality, and

my native land seems to

appear on my inner vision.

An ounce of moonlight

is worth a pound of gold.

回译

一盎司月光，一磅黄金

月光闪烁，明亮而

温柔，照入我的卧室；

于是，我从美梦之中，

轻轻醒来——发现

床前的地面上，如梦

似霜。我仰着愁苦之脸，

看向月亮，变得多愁

善感起来—— 故乡，

我的故乡，似乎

出现在我的心头

之上。一盎司月光，

抵得上，一磅黄金。

译人语

英译诗题 *An Ounce of Moonlight, a Pound of Gold*，具名言性质，而其汉语回译《一盎司月光，一磅黄金》却感觉缺少了英文的流畅度。翻译，有时总是无可奈何花落去，些许的遗憾，总是难免。译文中，英文 gently，使用两次；相应的汉语回译，却分别为"温柔"和"轻轻"，可谓同词而异译。短语 dreamily frosty，为偏正结构，对应的回译："如梦似霜"，却是平行结构。I gaze up at the moon with a stricken face in which there is much sentimentality，回译："我仰着愁苦之脸，看向月亮，变得多愁善感起来"，英文中，in which there is much sentimentality 是介词短语，做 a stricken face 的定语，汉语译文却分开处理。英文 my native land，回译"故乡，我的故乡"，重复"故乡"，只为抒情之故。

最后，An ounce of moonlight is worth a pound of gold，与标题类似，只是加上 is worth，变成了一个完整的句子。相应的回译："一盎司月光，抵得上，一磅黄金。"比读回译之诗题，也添加了"抵得上"。

望月之 88：Deep Night Moon: an Attack of Homesickness（深夜月：一阵乡思）

读英文

I'm slightly unwell, **an attack of dizziness**, I haven't been able to get up.

我感觉有点不舒服，一阵头晕，一直起不了床。

It was not until it was getting dark that evening that Gregor **awoke from his deep and coma-like sleep**.

直到黄昏时分，格雷戈尔才从深沉的昏睡中醒来。

The light from the electric street lamps shone palely here and there onto the ceiling and tops of the furniture, but down below, where Gregor was, it was dark.

街道上的电灯向四周散发出苍白的光，照射着天花板和家具的顶端，但是格雷戈尔所在的下面仍是一片黑暗。

A wolfish head, **wistful-eyed** and **frost-rimed**, thrust aside the tentflaps.

一颗狼一样的脑袋把帐篷的门帘顶到了一边，脑袋上的毛都结了一层白霜，眼中带着渴求的目光。

When **this underground town was lighted up by the bright rays thrown from the discs**, hung from the pillars and arches, its aspect was so strange, so fantastic, that it justified the praise of the guide-books, and visitors flocked to see it.

悬挂在柱子和拱顶上的电盘会发光，将这个地下城照亮，每当这时，它的样子便非常奇特、非常迷人，这也证明了旅行指南中的称赞名副其实。游客们

—271—

蜂拥而至。

The Swede moved heavily on his feet, re-examined the finger, then **turned an admiring gaze on the doctor**.

瑞典人挪动起他沉沉的步子，又检查了一下那根手指，然后向医生投以敬重的目光。

I think an immense deal of bonny Nell! A fine young creature like that, who has been brought up in the mine, is just the very wife for a miner.

我对美丽的内尔极为着迷！一个像她那样在煤矿中长大的年轻貌美的人，非常适合做一个矿工的妻子。

英文散译

Deep Night Moon: an Attack of Homesickness

I awake from my deep and coma-like sleep, by the moonlight shining here and there onto the frost-rimed floor before my bed. My little room is lighted up by the bright rays thrown from the moon, on which I turn an admiring gaze, and I begin to think an immense deal of my hometown — under an attack of homesickness.

英文诗译

Deep Night Moon: an Attack of Homesickness
I awake from my deep
and coma-like sleep, by the
moonlight shining here and
there onto the frost-rimed
floor before my bed. My
little room is lighted up by
the bright rays thrown from
the moon, on which I turn
an admiring gaze, and I begin
to think an immense deal
of my hometown — under
an attack of homesickness.

回译

深夜月：一阵乡思
我从深沉的昏睡
中醒来：在我床前
如敷白霜的地面上，
月光，四处闪烁。
我小小的卧室，
被一束束的光
照亮，来自月亮。
我向月亮投以欣赏
的眼光，然后开始
想家，想得疯狂——
一阵乡思，噢，
突袭我心头上。

译人语

英文译诗标题：*Deep Night Moon: an Attack of Homesickness*，汉语回译：《深夜月：一阵乡思》，基本对应。只是，英文名词 attack，为"攻击；袭击"之意，力度较大；汉语"一阵"，力度有所减小。不过，汉语回译的最后："一阵乡思，噢，突袭我心头上。"在"一阵乡思"之后，添加了"突袭我心头上"，终于与英文之力度，取得了旗鼓相当的效果。而且，添加的叹词"噢"，舒缓节奏，以助抒情。

英文译诗中，I begin to think an immense deal of my hometown，汉语回译："开始想家，想得疯狂"，译文首先低调处理："开始想家"，然后补充想家的力度："想得疯狂"。如此译法，可谓先抑后扬。整体而言，英文译诗由两个句子组成，汉语回译却包括三个句子。不拘一格，乃翻译之道。

望月之 89：The Height of Night, Moonrise & Homesickness（午夜，明月与乡愁共升）

读英文

It is **the height of summer**.
这里正值盛夏。

Bazin was then **at the height of joy**.
当时巴赞开心极了。

A dim light penetrated through the ventilating shaft **into** the glade.
一缕昏暗的光线从通风井渗进了空地。

The rest of the tent, sidewalls and top, **coated with a half-inch of dry, white, crystal-encrusted frost.**
帐篷剩下的部分，包括侧壁和顶棚，都罩着一层半寸厚的霜，又干又白，表面亮晶晶的。

At times like this **he would direct his eyes to the window and look out as clearly as he could**, but unfortunately, even the other side of the narrow street was enveloped in morning fog and **the view had little confidence or cheer to offer him.**
在这种时刻，他往往会将眼睛投向窗外，尽可能清楚地往外看。但不幸的是，连窄窄的街道的另一边都被晨雾包裹了，这种风景并没给他带来丝毫自信或是雀跃。

My internal being was in a state of insurrection and turmoil.
我的内心一直处于躁动不安的状态。

英文散译

The Height of Night, Moonrise & Homesickness

A silvery light penetrates through the window, into the room, onto the bedside floor, which seems to be coated with a film of white, crystal-encrusted frost. When I direct my eyes to the window and look out as clearly as I can, I find the view has much nostalgia to offer me — the height of night sees the height of moonrise, as well as the height of homesickness, as my internal being is in a state of turmoil.

英文诗译

The Height of Night, Moonrise & Homesickness

A silvery light penetrates through
the window, into the room, onto
the bedside floor, which seems to be
coated with a film of white, crystal-
encrusted frost. When I direct my
eyes to the window and look out
as clearly as I can, I find the view
has much nostalgia to offer me —
the height of night sees the height
of moonrise, as well as the height
of homesickness, as my internal
being is in a state of turmoil.

回译

午夜，明月与乡愁共升
一束银光，穿窗，
进入房间，落在
床前地上——似乎，
铺上了薄薄一层

亮晶晶的白霜。

我目光向窗，

往外张望，只见

景色依稀，牵动

乡愁——午夜，

明月与乡愁共升，

而我的心，也变得

不安，躁动……

译人语

译诗诗题：*The Height of Night, Moonrise & Homesickness*，其中，height 一词，英诗里常见，"高度；高处；顶点"之意；将 night, moonrise, homesickness 三词并置，笼于 height 之下，大有诗意。汉语回译：《午夜，明月与乡愁共升》，名词 height 虽好，翻译却难，于是，改用动词"共升"，以存其诗意。

借用的英文句子：A dim light penetrated through the ventilating shaft into the glade（一缕昏暗的光线从通风井渗进了空地），使用两个介词：through 和 into，句中没有逗号。其实，如果在 into 前加上逗号，也是可以的。不加，强调动作之连续。相应的汉语译文，也可以中间加上一个逗号："一缕昏暗的光线，从通风井渗进了空地"，或者："一缕昏暗的光线从通风井，渗进了空地"，当然，后者不如前者更好。借用之后，英文译诗里，介词 into 前，使用了逗号，以与随后的 onto 介词短语形成平行结构。

另外，the view has much nostalgia to offer me，借鉴自英文：the view had little confidence or cheer to offer him（这种风景并没给他带来丝毫自信或是雀跃），由否定变成肯定，成为好的英文表达。破折号之后，the height of night sees the height of moonrise, as well as the height of homesickness，三用 height，读者自然会回顾诗题：*The Height of Night, Moonrise & Homesickness*。其实，诗题，正是由此而来：先译出诗歌，再考虑诗之标题，也是译者常见的做法。从英文译诗到汉语回译，翻译手法同样多变。例如，the view has much nostalgia to offer me，回译"景色依稀，牵动乡愁"，文字并非拘泥；译诗最后，英文句号，中文却是省略号。

望月之 90：Utter Silence of the Night: Nostalgia Has Her Dwelling in My Heart （寂静之夜：乡愁，根植在我心上）

读英文

Again **in the utter silence** I heard that thin, sibilant note which spoke of intense suppressed excitement.

在一片静寂中，我又听到了那种细微的咝咝声，那是在努力忍住兴奋时才会发出的声响。

Misery had her dwelling in my heart, but I no longer talked in the same incoherent manner of my own crimes.

痛苦已根植在我的心中，但是我不再语无伦次地讲述自己的罪行。

The windows of the room had before been darkened, and I felt a kind of panic on **seeing the pale yellow light of the moon illuminate the chamber**.

房间的窗户先前是关着的，此刻，看到黯淡昏黄的月光照亮了房间，我感到了几分恐慌。

The only object that I could distinguish was the bright moon, and **I fixed my eyes on** that with pleasure.

我唯一能辨认的物体就是那皎洁的月亮，我满心欢喜地凝视着它。

He had passed a whole night in noting **the effect of the moonlight on** a silver image of Endymion.

他还曾熬通宵，观察月光照在恩底弥翁银像上产生的效果。

I can hardly describe to you the **effect** of these books. **They produced in me an infinity of new images and feelings, that sometimes raised me to ecstasy**, but more frequently **sunk me into the lowest dejection**.

我难以向你描述这些书对我产生的影响。它们令我的脑中出现了无数新形象和新感觉，有时令我如痴如醉，但更多的时候是让我陷入深深的沮丧。

英文散译

Utter Silence of the Night: Nostalgia Has Her Dwelling in My Heart

My chamber, in the utter silence of the night, is illuminated by the silvery light of the moon, which renders the bedside floor frostily white. I fix my wistful eyes through the lattice window on the moon, whose effect is instant: it produces in me an infinity of images of my homeland which raise me to ecstasy, before sinking me into the lowest dejection — nostalgia has her dwelling in my heart.

英文诗译

Utter Silence of the Night: Nostalgia Has Her Dwelling in My Heart

My chamber, in the utter silence
of the night, is illuminated by
the silvery light of the moon,
which renders the bedside floor
frostily white. I fix my wistful eyes
through the lattice window on
the moon, whose effect is instant:
it produces in me an infinity of
images of my homeland which raise
me to ecstasy, before sinking me into
the lowest dejection — nostalgia
has her dwelling in my heart.

回译

寂静之夜：乡愁，根植在我心上
卧室，在夜之寂

静中，被月之银光
点亮，使我床前地面，
银白如霜。我忧思
的目光，透过百叶
之窗，凝视着空中
的月亮——立刻，
我的脑海中，出现了
无数家乡的意象，
令我如痴如醉，让我
陷入深深的沮丧——
乡愁，根植在我心上。

译人语

英文介词短语 in the utter silence of the night，对应的汉语回译，诗中，"在夜之寂静中"，乃为直译，或忠实翻译；但在诗题中，却是"寂静之夜"，而不是"夜之寂静"，无它：只为通顺之故。另外，英文译诗开头：My chamber, in the utter silence of the night, is illuminated by the silvery light of the moon，借鉴自英文句子：I felt a kind of panic on seeing the pale yellow light of the moon illuminate the chamber.（看到黯淡昏黄的月光照亮了房间，我感到了几分恐慌。）英文用的是主动，借鉴后的译文，用的是被动，而且用了插入成分，因而似乎更有余味。汉语回译中，"被月之银光点亮"，不用"照亮"，而用"点亮"，也是为了诗意之故。译诗最后，nostalgia has her dwelling in my heart（乡愁，根植在我心上），部分重复了诗题，令人回味三咂。

望月之 91：The Moon Awakens My Homesickness（内心乡愁，月亮唤醒）

读英文

Porthos, at the sound of that voice, started like a man **awakened from a sleep of a hundred years**.

听见这声音，波尔托就像刚刚从一百年的沉睡中惊醒一样。

I was still stupid from our yesterday's debauch.

昨晚我们的放纵让我还迷迷糊糊的。

And immediately two swords **glittered in the rays of the setting sun**, and the combat began with an animosity very natural to men who were enemies.

刹那间，两只剑在落日的余辉下闪闪发光，敌人相见分外眼红，一场激战开始了。

"Good Lord, how quickly men forget!" cried the procurator's wife, **raising her eyes toward heaven**.

"老天，男人是多么健忘啊！"律师夫人仰头望着天大声说道。

Ah, you begin **to awaken my regret**.

啊，听你这么一说，我又开始后悔了。

The tale was quickly told, but **it awakened various trains of reflection**.

我的经历三言两语就讲完了，但这唤起了千丝万缕的回忆。

But **her thoughts were far away, across** the Ice Mountains **to the east, to the**

little corner of the earth where her childhood had been lived.

　　但是她的思绪飘得很远，穿过冰山去了东方，去了那个她儿时生活过的角落。

英文散译

The Moon Awakens My Homesickness

　　I am awakened, by a slanting beam of light, from a sound sleep from which I am still stupid — my bed-side floor is glittering like silvery frost in the rays of the moon, which I see as I raise my eyes toward heaven. The moon awakens my homesickness and various trains of reflection — my thoughts are far away, across hills and rills upon hills and rills, to the little corner of the earth where my childhood has been lived.

英文诗译

The Moon Awakens My Homesickness

I am awakened, by a slanting beam
of light, from a sound sleep from
which I am still stupid — my bedside floor is glittering like silvery
frost in the rays of the moon,
which I see as I raise my eyes
toward heaven. The moon awakens
my homesickness and various trains
of reflection — my thoughts are far
away, across hills and rills upon hills
and rills, to the little corner of the earth
where my childhood has been lived.

回译

　　内心乡愁，月亮唤醒
　　斜斜的一束亮光，
　　把我从睡梦中照醒，

我仍在恍惚之中——
抬眼望天，只见一轮
明月，闪烁于床前的
地面：如银，似霜。
我内心的乡愁，被月亮
唤醒，也唤醒了我千丝
万缕的回忆——我的
思绪，飞跃万水千山，
来到地球这小小的角落：
我度过童年的地方。

译人语

英文诗题 *The Moon Awakens My Homesickness*，若回译汉语《月亮唤醒了我的乡愁》，则平淡而没有诗意，现译为《内心乡愁，月亮唤醒》，采用倒装，效果稍好。英文译诗第三行中的 stupid，非"愚蠢的"，而是"神思恍惚的"之意。接下来，第五行中的介词 in，词小而精妙。"读英文"第三句：And immediately two swords glittered in the rays of the setting sun, and the combat began with an animosity very natural to men who were enemies.（刹那间，两只剑在落日的余辉下闪闪发光, 敌人相见分外眼红, 一场激战开始了。）其中, two swords glittered in the rays of the setting sun，对应的汉语译文："两只剑在落日下闪闪发光"。仔细看来，介词用的是 in，不是 under；因此，"余辉下"，属于意译；如果直译，当为"余辉里"。汉语当然不能当真使用"余辉里"，而英文的 in，何其漂亮！借用之后，英文译诗：my bed-side floor is glittering like silvery frost in the rays of the moon，这里的介词 in，具相同之美学效果。

译诗第八行中的 train，非"列车；火车"之意，而是表示"行列；一系列"。译诗最后，where my childhood has been lived，动词 lived，也可以改成 spent。例如，"望月之 75"的最后：the moon always shines as the compass of my life, wherever it is spent，这里的 it，指 life，而 life 与 childhood 性质类同。

望月之 92：Silence & Night & Nostalgia （静·夜·思）

读英文

Day **began to appear at the window-blinds,** and soon **invaded the chamber with its pallid light**.

晨光透过窗帘，把微弱的光线洒进房间里。

A becoming dress **lends charm to** a girl.

合身的衣服给一个女子增加美。

And M. de Treville, who **detected** him **at once**.

而德特雷维尔先生也一眼看到了他。

The cardinal **fixed his keen eyes on** the bold speaker.

红衣主教用敏锐的目光注视着这个勇敢的回话者。

Milady looked at her lover **in silence**.

米拉迪默不作声地看着她的情人。

Athos walked about in **a contemplative mood**.

阿托斯则沉思着踱来踱去。

There was a moment when he **felt something like** remorse.

他心里有一刹那的愧疚。

He **felt something like a secret joy** at being for ever rid of such a dangerous accomplice.

能够摆脱这样一个危险的同谋，他隐约感到一种窃喜。

英文散译

Silence & Night & Nostalgia

The moon begins to appear at the window-blinds, and soon invades the chamber with its silvery light, which lends frosty stuff to the floor. I detect at once, without the window, the ice wheel, on which I fix my eyes in silence, and I am reduced to a contemplative mood, feeling something like nostalgia.

英文诗译

Silence & Night & Nostalgia

The moon begins to appear
at the window-blinds, and
soon invades the chamber
with its silvery light,
which lends frosty stuff
to the floor. I detect at
once, without the window,
the ice wheel, on which I
fix my eyes in silence,
and I am reduced to a
contemplative mood, feeling
something like nostalgia.

回译

静 · 夜 · 思
月光透过窗帘，
把银色的光线
洒进房间，
给地面敷上霜
也似的东西。
窗外，我一眼
就看到一个冰轮，

我注视着她，
静悄悄地——
我开始沉思，
并感到一种
乡愁的滋味。

译人语

英文诗题 *Silence & Night & Nostalgia*，使用了英文常用的表示并列的符号 &，很有意思。汉语回译：《静·夜·思》，用汉语常见的点号，来对等英文符号，而且，这与李白之原题《静夜思》完全一致，只是添加了点号而已；这就延缓了阅读之节奏，正符合《静夜思》之情绪。

译诗中，使用 window-blinds（窗帘），不同于"窗户"，更加具象而已。动词 invade，汉译"洒进"，只达其意，不传其力；英文 invade 太过形象，汉语似无可奈何。随后，frosty stuff（霜也似的东西），恰吻合"疑是地上霜"之内在含义。另外，译诗中，用 the ice wheel（冰轮）来指代月亮，对于英文或中文读者而言，都不难理解。

望月之 93：The Tender Moon Is Shining on in the Calmness of the Night（静谧之夜，柔情之月依然亮）

读英文

The little soft light **shone on in the calmness of the night**.
在静谧的夜色中，那柔和的灯光依然亮着。

The three blows were scarcely struck when the inside casement was opened, and **a light appeared through the panes of the shutter.**
刚敲过三下，里面的那层窗子就打开了，灯光从百叶窗的缝隙里透了出来。

The sparrow **alighted on** a nearby branch.
那支麻雀飞落在附近的树枝上。

On either hand the sun-dogs blazed. **The air was a gossamer of glittering frost**.
日晕两侧，幻日闪耀。空气好像璀璨霜花结成的薄纱。

He lay on his armor-like back, and if **he lifted his head a little** he could see his brown belly, slightly domed and divided by arches into stiff sections.
他躺在盔甲般的背上，稍一抬头就可以看到棕色的、微微鼓起、被一条条拱形分成僵硬的小块的肚皮。

In an instant he was among the branches, and **his keen eyes plunged through**

the transparent panes into the interior of the pavilion.

一眨眼的功夫他就站到了枝杈间，热切的眼睛穿过透明的玻璃窗，看到了小楼里边。

The remembrance of the scene at St. Germain **presented itself to the mind of** the presumptuous Gascon.

圣热尔曼的那场搏斗，立马又浮现在这位自以为是的加斯科涅人的脑海里。

英文散译

The Tender Moon Is Shining on in the Calmness of the Night

A light appears through the panes of the shutter, before alighting on the floor before my bed — the air is a gossamer of glittering frost. I lift my head a little, my keen eyes plunging through the semi-transparent panes into the night sky, where the tender moon is shining on in the calmness of the night, and the remembrance of the scene in my beloved homeland presents itself to my mind.

英文诗译

The Tender Moon Is Shining on in the Calmness of the Night

A light appears through the panes
of the shutter, before alighting on
the floor before my bed — the air
is a gossamer of glittering frost.
I lift my head a little, my keen
eyes plunging through the semi-
transparent panes into the night sky,
where the tender moon is
shining on in the calmness of
the night, and the remembrance
of the scene in my beloved homeland presents itself to my mind.

回译

静谧之夜，柔情之月依然亮
一束光，从百叶窗
的缝隙透了进来，
然后落在我床前的
地上——空气好像
璀璨霜花结成的薄纱。
我稍微抬头，热切的
眼睛穿过半透明的
玻璃窗，看向夜空——
静谧之夜，柔情之月
依然亮。我那可爱家乡
的情景，被重新忆起，
浮现在我的脑海里。

译人语

"读英文"第一句：The little soft light shone on in the calmness of the night. （在静谧的夜色中，那柔和的灯光依然亮着。）其中，on 是副词，"继续"之意，修饰之前的 shone；in 是介词，搭配其后的 calmness。英文译诗标题借鉴于此，因有 *The Tender Moon Is Shining on in the Calmness of the Night*。其中的 tender，又英文句中的 soft 联想开来，又想到美国作家 Francis Scott Fitzgerald 的名著 *Tender Is the Night*，既然 night 可以 tender，月亮为何不可呢？诗题回译：《静谧之夜，柔情之月依然亮》，显然，将 the Calmness of the Night 倒装，翻译成了"静谧之夜"，而不是"夜之静谧"；否则，无法做"柔情之月依然亮"的时间状语。

接下来的译文中，介词 before，看似简单，其实地道；对应的汉语译文，往往是"然后"。其实，找遍任何英汉词典，都没有把 before 解释为"然后"的，根据上下文语境的翻译而已。随后，the air is a gossamer of glittering frost，直接借鉴自英文，只是把时态由一般过去时改成一般现在时而已：用 is 来代替 was。随后的译文，还有几处亮点：my keen eyes plunging through the semi-transparent panes into the night sky，其中动词 plunge（使投入；跳入；栽进；下降，急降，突降），出人意表，生动形象，也是借鉴英文的结果；presents itself to my mind 中，反身代词的使用，发挥了英文的优势，英文善用反身代词，多生动传神。另外，译文中，the tender moon is shining on in the calmness of the night，完全重复了诗题；汉语回译：《静谧之夜，柔情之月依然亮》，亦随之而重复。

望月之 94：The Deeps of Sleep, the Deeps of Homesickness（梦之酣时，乡思亦酣）

读英文

It was a cry that began, muffled, **in the deeps of sleep**, that swiftly rushed upward.

这一叫喊声刚开始时是沉睡中的低声嘟囔，接着很快提高了声调。

The lane was still deserted, and **the same calm soft light shone through the window**.

小巷依然空荡荡的，从那扇窗户里照出来的还是柔和的灯光。

Further, this woman, as if not certain of the house she was seeking, **lifted up her eyes to look around her,** stopped, went a little back, and then returned again.

而且，那个女人似乎不知道自己要找的到底是哪个屋子。她不断抬头环视四周，走走停停，折回去，又倒回来。

All eyes were fixed upon the yawning mouth of the Columbiad.

所有的眼睛都紧紧地盯着哥伦比亚大炮的巨大炮口。

She eyed it **wistfully**, grasping its virtues at a glance and thrilling again at the unaccountable sensations it aroused.

她渴望地看着那木屋，一下就明白了它的好处，那些无法言喻的感受又令她激动起来。

On the sixteenth day **signs of anxiety were so manifest in D'Artagnan and his three friends that** they could not remain quiet in one place.

第十六天，达塔尼昂和三位朋友脸上满是焦虑，他们简直无法在某个地方安静地呆上一会儿。

I doubt if he can have **retained a very clear recollection of me**.
我怀疑他是否还清楚地记得我。

There was one other memory of the past, dim and faded, but **stamped into his soul everlasting** by the savage feet of his father.

关于过去的记忆里还有一件事，虽然有些模糊不清了，但他父亲那双野蛮的脚还是永远铭刻在了他的灵魂深处。

英文散译

The Deeps of Sleep, the Deeps of Homesickness

I am awakened from the deeps of sleep, by a calm soft light shining through the window, before I lift up my eyes to look around me, to find the floor silvered with a thin film of frost. When I glance and fix my gaze upon the moon wistfully, there are instant signs of homesickness so manifest in me that I retain a very clear recollection of my hometown life — there are so many fond memories of the past, dim and faded, yet stamped into my soul everlastingly.

英文诗译

The Deeps of Sleep, the Deeps of Homesickness
I am awakened from the deeps
of sleep, by a calm soft light
shining through the window,
before I lift up my eyes to
look around me, to find the
floor silvered with a thin
film of frost. When I glance
and fix my gaze upon the moon

wistfully, there are instant signs
of homesickness so manifest
in me that I retain a very clear
recollection of my hometown
life — there are so many
fond memories of the past,
dim and faded, yet stamped
into my soul everlastingly.

回译

梦之酣时，乡思亦酣
一束静柔之光，
穿窗而入——
我从酣睡中醒来，
抬眼环顾四周，
只见地面镀银：
一层薄薄的白霜。
举目遥望，我
盯着月亮，眼里
满含着渴望，
脸上满溢着乡愁
——家乡的生活，
依然清晰如昨——
诸多甜美的回忆，
虽然模糊迷离，
却永远铭刻在
我灵魂的深处。

译人语

英文译诗标题：*The Deeps of Sleep, the Deeps of Homesickness*，借鉴自英
文句子：It was a cry that began, muffled, in the deeps of sleep, that swiftly rushed

upward.（这一叫喊声刚开始时是沉睡中的低声嘟囔，接着很快提高了声调。）作为 deep 的复数，deeps 的词典释义为："深处；深渊"。标题回译：《梦之酣时，乡思亦酣》，原译是《梦之酣时，思乡亦酣》。"乡思"与"思乡"，同字而异序，效果大不相同。"思乡"，为动词，或者动词含义明显，而之前的"梦"，显为名词，表示静态之意。因此，把动词"思乡"，改为"乡思"，作为名词，便与名词之"梦"对上：节奏平稳。

译诗中，介词 by，表示被动语态，回译未用"被"字，而用一破折号，效果颇佳：不仅暗示了被动之意，还令人联想到月光透入房间的状貌。稍后，…wistfully, there are instant signs of homesickness so manifest in me，对应汉语回译："眼里满含着渴望，脸上满溢着乡愁"，英文句散，汉语句整。深度理解之后，打破原文之格局，重新组句，也是翻译之常态。译文最后：there are so many fond memories of the past, dim and faded, yet stamped into my soul everlastingly，借鉴自英文句子：There was one other memory of the past, dim and faded, but stamped into his soul everlasting by the savage feet of his father.（关于过去的记忆里还有一件事，虽然有些模糊不清了，但他父亲那双野蛮的脚还是永远铭刻在了他的灵魂深处。）原文 everlasting，为形容词，不知何故。为保险起见，译文改用副词 everlastingly，用来修饰动词 stamp。从标点符号来看，英文译诗中，常见的逗号句号之外，还有一个破折号；汉语回译中，逗号句号之外，还有一个冒号和三个破折号。相较于英语，汉语似乎更加善用标点。

望月之 95：Still Night, My Hometown Is My Whole Thought, My Whole Soul （静深之夜，我的故乡，是我全部的思想，整个的灵魂）

读英文

This woman **was already his whole thought, his whole soul**.
这个女人已经操控了他的全部思想和灵魂。

No light shone through the chinks of the shutters; no sound gave reason to believe that it was inhabited. It was dark and silent as a tomb.
窗缝中没有透出一丝光，也没有一点声音，让人感觉这座房子无人居住。它如同一座坟墓般漆黑寂静。

She leaned with one hand on the arm of the chair, and **protruded her head as if to** meet a certainty.
她一只手撑在椅子扶手上，伸着头，似乎要确定一下这个人是谁。

Milady **gazed with all her eyes**; it was just light enough for her to recognize those who were coming.
米拉迪聚精会神地注视着，天色尚明，足以使她辨认出来者是谁。

Milady **felt her soul bathed in a hellish joy**.
米拉迪感到自己的灵魂沉浸在邪恶的欢乐中。

英文散译

Still Night, My Hometown Is My Whole Thought, My Whole Soul

Light is shining through the chinks of the shutters before flowing onto the frosty floor, as I protrude my head to ascertain that it is the light of the moon, at which I gaze with all my eyes, and I feel my soul bathed in a comforting joy. And my hometown — my hometown is already my whole thought, my whole soul.

英文诗译

Still Night, My Hometown Is My Whole Thought, My Whole Soul

Light is shining through
the chinks of the shutters
before flowing onto the
frosty floor, as I protrude
my head to ascertain that
it is the light of the moon,
at which I gaze with all
my eyes, and I feel my soul
bathed in a comforting joy.
And my hometown —
my hometown is already my
whole thought, my whole soul.

回译

静深之夜，我的故乡，是我全部的思想，整个的灵魂
窗缝中，透出
一丝光，随后
流到如霜的地上，
我探头，确认这
就是月亮之光——
我聚精会神地凝望，
感觉自己的灵魂

沉浸在令人慰藉
的欢乐中。故乡——
我的故乡，是我
全部的思想，
整个的灵魂。

译人语

英文译诗标题：*Still Night, My Hometown Is My Whole Thought, My Whole Soul*，汉语回译：《静深之夜，我的故乡，是我全部的思想，整个的灵魂》，直译出之：虽然繁琐，却不乏诗意。译诗开头：Light is shining through the chinks of the shutters before flowing onto the frosty floor（窗缝中，透出一丝光，随后流到如霜的地上），把月光比喻成流水，大好。唐诗中，多有流水之意象，以喻明月，如："月光如水水如天"（赵嘏《江楼感旧》）。随后，英文 the light of the moon（月亮之光），虽然冗长，却不能用 moonlight（月光）代替，因为这光需要 ascertain（确认），毕竟，"疑是地上霜"的嘛。英文句子：Milady felt her soul bathed in a hellish joy.（米拉迪感到自己的灵魂沉浸在邪恶的欢乐中。）将形容词 hellish 改为 comforting，以符合月光给人带来的慰藉之感；同时，改变人称和时态，便有译文：I feel my soul bathed in a comforting joy（感觉自己的灵魂沉浸在令人慰藉的欢乐中），正是《静夜思》的深层之译。最后，And my hometown — my hometown is already my whole thought, my whole soul，回译："故乡——我的故乡，是我全部的思想，整个的灵魂。"其中，my hometown 完全重复，"故乡"与"我的故乡"，却是部分重复；whole 复用，汉译却分而治之："全部的"与"整个的"。翻译，乃化学，总要变化，以适应不同的语境。

望月之 96：A Deep Reverie in a Deep Night（**静夜沉思**）

读英文

Athos **fell into a deep reverie** and made no remark.
阿托斯却陷入沉思之中，未做回应。

And as at that moment **all was silence in** the old castle.
此时，整个古堡一片寂静，只听到海浪永恒的低吟。

The rent is **inclusive of** water and heating.
租金包括水费和暖气费。

But whether this was **reality or vision**, he had this time sufficient self-command not to enter.

但不管这是真的还是幻觉，这一次，费尔顿竟然能够控制住自己没有进屋。

She **fell into a reverie about her childhood**.
她沉浸在对童年往事的遐想中。

Grimaud silently swallowed the glass of Bordeaux wine; but **his eyes, raised toward heaven during the whole time this delicious occupation lasted, spoke a language which, though mute, was none the less expressive**.

格里莫默默地喝下了那杯波尔多葡萄酒。在享受这杯美酒的过程中，他的眼睛始终望着天空，这种无声的语言同样富有表现力。

Then she continued her singing **with inexpressible fervor and feeling**. It appeared to her that the sounds spread to a distance beneath the vaulted roofs, and **carried with them a magic charm to soften the hearts** of her jailers.

然后她以一种难以言表的热忱和情感继续吟唱。她觉得她的声音沿着穹顶飘到远方。这声音带着一种魔力，去软化她的狱卒的心。

Fascinated by this strange creature, he could not **detach his eyes from her eyes**. 似乎被这个奇特的生灵所吸引，无法把目光从这个女人的眼睛上移开。

英文散译

A Deep Reverie in a Deep Night

All is silence in the little room, inclusive of an ethereal film of frost on the floor before my bed — is it reality or vision? I fall into a deep reverie about my childhood as my eyes, raised toward heaven during the whole time this reverie lasts, speak a language which, though mute, is none the less expressive. When I watch the moon with inexpressible fervor and feeling, it seems the moon carries with it a magic charm to soften my heart and, for a great while, I fail to detach my eyes from the moon.

英文诗译

A Deep Reverie in a Deep Night
All is silence in the little room,
inclusive of an ethereal film
of frost on the floor before my
bed — is it reality or vision?
I fall into a deep reverie about
my childhood as my eyes,
raised toward heaven during
the whole time this reverie lasts,
speak a language which, though
mute, is none the less expressive.
When I watch the moon with
inexpressible fervor and feeling,

it seems the moon carries with it
a magic charm to soften my heart
and, for a great while, I fail to
detach my eyes from the moon.

回译

静夜沉思
小小的卧室里，一片寂静，
包括床前地面上一层
薄薄的、若有似无的缥缈
白霜——真实存在？亦或
幻觉使然？我陷入沉思，
沉浸在对童年往事的
遐想之中——我的眼睛，
始终凝视着天空，这种
无声的语言，同样富有
表现力。当我看着月亮 ——
以一种难以言表的热忱
和情感——似乎月亮
带有一种魔力，来软化
我的心；并且，时间久长，
我无法移开，从月亮上
移开——我的目光。

译人语

英文译诗标题 *A Deep Reverie in a Deep Night*，借鉴自英文句子：Athos fell into a deep reverie and made no remark.（阿托斯却陷入沉思之中，未做回应。）从中借来 a deep reverie 的组合，再加上 in a deep night 的添加，复用 deep，感觉良好。译诗中，is it reality or vision?（真实存在？亦或幻觉使然？）生动形象地译出了"疑是地上霜"之"疑"字。接着，I fall into a deep reverie about my childhood，译文重复了诗题中的 a deep reverie，随后，as my eyes, raised toward heaven during the whole time this reverie lasts, speak a language which, though mute, is none the less expressive.（我的眼睛，始终凝视着天空，这种无声的语言，同样富有表现力。）直接借鉴自英文，表达虽繁琐而不失韵味。下一个句子同样极富韵致：When I watch the moon with inexpressible fervor and feeling, it seems the moon carries with it a magic charm to soften my heart and, for a great while, I fail to detach my eyes from the moon.（当我看着月亮——以一种难以言表的热忱和情感——似乎月亮带有一种魔力，来软化我的心；并且，时间久长，我无法移开，从月亮上移开——我的目光。）比读汉语回译，感觉还是英文更好，更有余味。阅读并借鉴英文文学作品里的言语方式，是提高汉诗英译质量的一个有效途径。

望月之 97：Solitary Midnight: a Burst of Inward Pining for Home（**孤独的午夜：内心迸发出思乡的渴望**）

读英文

What hatred she distills! Motionless, with her burning and fixed glances, **in her solitary apartment**, how well **the outbursts of passion** which at times **escape from the depths of her chest** with her respiration, accompany the sound of the surf which rises, growls, roars, and breaks itself like an eternal and powerless despair against the rocks on which is built this dark and lofty castle!

她积蓄了多少憎恨啊！她一动不动地站在那里，目光如炬，紧盯着自己孤零零的牢房，随着呼吸不时从胸腔中迸发出激愤，伴着不断起伏、怒吼、咆哮的海浪。那海浪仿佛陷入永恒而无力的绝望之中，狠狠地向着垒起这座黑暗、高耸的城堡的岩石撞去！

…burying herself under the clothes to conceal from anybody who might be watching her **this burst of inward satisfaction**.

为了不让任何人发现自己内心迸发出的满足，米拉迪把整个身子埋进了被子里。

One window was lighted.
一扇窗户里透出灯光。

She **cast her eyes upon** the table, saw the glittering of a knife.

她将目光投向桌子，看见一把刀在桌上闪闪发光。

And he **let his head sink into his hands**, while two tears rolled down his cheeks.

说完，达塔尼昂把自己的头埋入双手，两行眼泪从脸颊滚落。

"You are young," replied Athos, "and **your bitter recollections have time to be changed into sweet memories**."

"你还年轻，"阿托斯说，"你还有时间把苦涩模糊的回忆变成甜蜜的记忆。"

英文散译

Solitary Midnight: a Burst of Inward Pining for Home

The window is lighted, and the floor before my bed is silvery with a seemingly thin film of frost. The solitary room sees an outburst of passion which escapes from the depths of my chest, as well as a burst of inward pining for home, as I cast my eyes upon the midnight moon without the window in the boundless blue sky, and I let my head sink into my hands — with the passage of time, the bitter recollections have been changed into sweet memories.

英文诗译

Solitary Midnight: a Burst of Inward Pining for Home

The window is lighted, and
the floor before my bed is
silvery with a seemingly thin
film of frost. The solitary
room sees an outburst of
passion which escapes
from the depths of my chest,
as well as a burst of inward
pining for home, as I cast my
eyes upon the midnight moon
without the window in the

boundless blue sky, and I let
my head sink into my hands —
with the passage of time, the
bitter recollections have been
changed into sweet memories.

回译

孤独的午夜：内心迸发出思乡的渴望
窗户里透进亮光，
我床前的地面，
闪烁如银，似乎
着上了一层薄霜。
孤零零的房间里，
我的胸腔，涌动着
激情，内心迸发出
思乡的渴望。我
将目光投向窗外
之月——正悬于无边
的蓝色夜空。然后，
我把自己的头埋入
双手——随着时间
的流逝，那些苦涩
模糊的记忆，早已
变成甜蜜的回忆。

译人语

英文译诗标题：*Solitary Midnight: a Burst of Inward Pining for Home*，汉语回译《孤独的午夜：内心迸发出思乡的渴望》，算是对等之直译。标题较长，尤其相比于原诗三字之《静夜思》，不过，也算是古诗标题之当代诗意阐释。借鉴英文之后，英文译诗多个语言亮点，如 an outburst of passion which escapes from the depths of my chest，a burst of inward pining for home，I let my head sink into my hands 等。另外，译诗最后：with the passage of time, the bitter recollections have been changed into sweet memories.（随着时间的流逝，那些苦涩模糊的回忆，早已变成甜蜜的记忆。）李白之《静夜思》并未如此描写，而人生到了一定程度，或许就难免类似的感悟。

整体观之，英文译诗由两个句子构成，一个短句，一个长句；汉语回译却是四个句子。英语喜欢长句，汉语喜欢短句，不太常见很长的句子。因此，翻译教科书中，谈到翻译技巧，总会谈到英语长句的拆分译法。

望月之 98：The Placid Moon & a Perfect Longing for Home（恬静之月·思乡之苦）

读英文

The fact is that I felt as though I were choking and **had a perfect longing for** a breath of fresh air.

事实上，我觉得好像有点儿气闷，特别想出去呼吸下新鲜空气。

It was on a bitterly cold and **frosty morning** during the winter of '97 that **I was awakened by** a tugging at my shoulder.

那是 1897 年的冬天，一个严寒霜冻的黎明，有人推我的肩膀，把我叫醒。

Richelieu **looked steadfastly at** the young man.

黎塞留一动不动地盯着这个年轻人。

The light burned dimly and steadily and he had the feel that it was a sick-room.

灯光暗淡平稳，他感觉那是间病房。

When I came to England I was **as perfect a stranger to all the world as if** I had never been known there.

当我重返英国时，对于所有的人已经完全是一个陌生人了，就像那里从来没人认识我一样。

For the next two months, life in the village went its **placid** way.

接下来的两个月，村中的生活一如既往的平静。

英文散译

The Placid Moon & a Perfect Longing for Home

A frosty night, I am awakened by a splash of light which coats the bedside floor in silvery rime. I look steadfastly at the moon without the window, which shines brilliantly and steadily, and I have a perfect longing for home. The strange room, the strange floor, the strange bed — all give me a feeling that I am a perfect stranger to all the world here, except the familiar placid moon.

英文诗译

The Placid Moon & a Perfect Longing for Home
A frosty night, I am awakened
by a splash of light which coats
the bedside floor in silvery rime.
I look steadfastly at the moon
without the window, which shines
brilliantly and steadily, and I have
a perfect longing for home.
The strange room, the strange
floor, the strange bed — all give
me a feeling that I am a perfect
stranger to all the world here,
except the familiar placid moon.

回译

恬静之月·思乡之苦
一个严寒霜冻的晚上，
我被一束闪烁之光晃醒，
光照地上，如银似霜。
我一动不动地盯着窗外
之月：其光灿烂、匀恒，
我开始饱尝乡思之苦。

陌生的卧室，陌生的
地面，陌生的床啊——
给我一种感觉：在这个
地方，异域他乡，我整个儿
就是陌生之人——除了，
那熟悉而恬静的 ——月亮。

译人语

英文诗题 *The Placid Moon & a Perfect Longing for Home*，两个名词性短语并列，汉语回译《恬静之月·思乡之苦》如法炮制，均具诗意。译文中，which shines brilliantly and steadily（其光灿烂、匀恒），借鉴自英文句子：The light burned dimly and steadily and he had the feel that it was a sick room.（灯光暗淡平稳，他感觉那是间病房。）由主语 light，想到 the moon，由动词 burn，想到与月亮搭配的 shine，由 dimly and steadily，想到前者的反义词，改成：brilliantly and steadily。借鉴英文之时，有时几乎照搬即可，有时需要这样的改动，有时的改动，比这个还大，视情况而定。随后的译文：I have a perfect longing for home，回译可为："我特别想家"，但无法打通译文前后，于是改成："我开始饱尝乡思之苦"，终于前后衔接无缝，语言也更具雅味。

汉语回译："陌生的卧室，陌生的地面，陌生的床啊"，加上"啊"字，就避免的单字"床"的失衡，也有抒情之韵味。随后，英文 to all the world here，不可当真译成"这里的整个世界"：其实指的是我所客居的这个地方。因此，回译："在这个地方，异域他乡"，一语双译，暗含无奈与叹息。紧随其后的回译，"整个儿"、"陌生之人"等，措语考究；"——除了，那熟悉而恬静的——月亮"，其中标点，用心，而表情。

望月之 99：Meditation in the Quietude of the Night（夜深人静沉思时）

读英文

He was often thus when communing with himself on board ship **in the quietude of the night**.

每当夜深人静，他在船上暗自思量时，总是如此。

He was accompanied by a strange light, no bigger than your fist, which darted about the room like a living thing and I think it must have been **this light that wakened Mrs. Darling**.

一簇奇怪的光伴着他，那光不比你的拳头大，却仿佛有生命似的在屋子里到处蹿动，我猜，肯定是这簇光把达林夫人弄醒了。

He awoke in the morning to find a piping gale from the south.
他早晨醒来的时候，大风从南边呼啸着刮过来。

It was still shut, but the room **was ablaze with light.**
窗户还是关着的，但屋里却一片光亮。

A dim light crept through the windows of the pagoda.
昏暗的光束小心翼翼地穿出寺庙的窗户。

The sunlight streamed placidly over the town.
阳光宁静地洒在这个小镇上。

Fix, seated in the bow, **gave himself up to meditation.**

菲克斯坐在船头沉思着。

He had a vision of himself being found dead in the snow, and for a while he wept in self-pity.

他想象着自己被人发现死在雪地里，自怜地哭了好一会儿。

It happened to be Nana's evening off, and Mrs. Darling had bathed them and sung to them till one by one they had let go her hand and **slid away into the land of sleep**.

娜娜碰巧在那天晚上休息，达林夫人给孩子们洗澡，唱歌给他们听，直到他们一个接一个地松开了她的手，进入了梦乡。

英文散译

Meditation in the Quietude of the Night

I am wakened in the quietude of the night by a shaft of light to find the floor shiveringly ablaze with a thin coat of rime, before I direct my eyes to the window, to detect a view which has much cheer to offer me — a bright moonlight creeps through the window, streaming placidly into the room. I give myself up to meditation, while having a vision of myself being transported back to my land of home, to my land of comfort, to my land of rest and sleep.

英文诗译

Meditation in the Quietude of the Night

I am wakened in the quietude
of the night by a shaft of light
to find the floor shiveringly
ablaze with a thin coat of
rime, before I direct my eyes
to the window, to detect a
view which has much cheer
to offer me — a bright moonlight creeps through the
window, streaming placidly

into the room. I give myself
up to meditation, while having
a vision of myself being
transported back to my land
of home, to my land of comfort,
to my land of rest and sleep.

回译

夜深人静沉思时
夜深人静，一簇
亮光把我照醒，
只见床前地面
明晃晃：似乎
敷了一层薄霜。
然后，我注目看窗，
发现景色正开朗
——一轮明月，
小心翼翼钻入窗，
月光宁静，如水
洒在地面上。
我沉思，想象着
自己，魂飞魄翔，
回故乡——我
那安乐之乡，
恬静美梦之乡。

译人语

英诗译文中，I direct my eyes to the window, to detect a view which has much cheer to offer me，借鉴自英文句子：At times like this he would direct his eyes to the window and look out as clearly as he could, but unfortunately, even the other side of the narrow street was enveloped in morning fog and the view had little confidence or cheer to offer him.（在这种时刻，他往往会将眼睛投向窗外，尽可能清楚地往外看。但不幸的是，连窄窄的街道的另一边都被晨雾包裹了，这种风景并没给他带来丝毫自信或是雀跃。）这个句子在"望月之 89"中出现过，因此，不出现在"读英文"中。但此处借鉴，仍为译文出彩之处，因此，复述于此。

诗题：*Meditation in the Quietude of the Night*，回译：《夜深人静沉思时》，加一"时"字，而一时有味。译文中，in the quietude of the night 和 meditation，均有重复，只是分而散之，仍有题文呼应之效果。汉语回译中，"魂飞魄翔"，改写自成语"魂飞魄散"，一字之差，完全不同。其实，改写源于"飞翔"，将两字分开，成为"魂飞"、"魄翔"，也就是"魂魄飞翔"之意，对应英文 myself being transported back to，属于洒脱之译。译诗最后，to my land of home, to my land of comfort, to my land of rest and sleep，三用 to my land of，后接 home，comfort，rest and sleep，层层递进，分别表示"家乡"、"舒服或安乐之乡"、"休息和睡眠之乡"；相应的汉语回译："回故乡——我那安乐之乡，恬静美梦之乡"，稍事雅化而成。如此结尾，似与苏轼有了心灵感应，其词《定风波·南海归赠王定国侍人寓娘》云："此心安处是吾乡"，一叹。

望月之 100：Quiet Night Homesickness（静夜乡思）

读英文

The sea was like oil, **the moon shone in all splendor**, and the Shark continued to sleep so soundly that not even a cannon shot would have awakened him.

海水就像油一样发亮，月亮发出盈盈光芒，而鲨鱼还在继续沉睡着，甚至连大炮都吵不醒它。

The moonlight **bathed the scene in silver**.

月光把一切镀成了银色。

Then came the meagre breakfast, the tramp through the dark, and the pale **glimpse of** day across the housetops as he turned his back on it and went in through the factory gate.

吃过寒酸的早饭，他摸黑赶路，房顶上曙光暗淡，他转身走进工厂的大门。

She eyed it **wistfully**, grasping its virtues at a glance and **thrilling again at the unaccountable sensations it aroused**.

她渴望地看着那木屋，一下就明白了它的好处，那些无法言喻的感受又令她激动起来。

A certain feeling of independence crept up in him, and the relationship between him and his mother changed.

他萌生了某种自食其力的感觉，接着他和母亲的关系开始发生了变化。

英文散译

Quiet Night Homesickness

The moon, shining in all splendor, is bathing my bedside floor in silver, suggestive of hoarfrost. A glimpse of the moon, wistfully, through the lattice window, and I am thrilling at the unaccountable sensations it arouses, when homesickness is creeping up in me.

英文诗译

Quiet Night Homesickness

The moon, shining
in all splendor, is bathing
my bedside floor in
silver, suggestive of
hoarfrost. A glimpse
of the moon, wistfully,
through the lattice window,
and I am thrilling at
the unaccountable
sensations it arouses,
when homesickness
is creeping up in me.

回译

静夜乡思
月儿，闪亮——
盈盈光芒，镀银
我床前的地板
之上，令人想起
冷霜。搭眼望见
月亮，心生渴望，
透过花格之窗，

我亢奋昂扬——
月亮勾人魂魄，
情深无处宣扬；
静夜乡思难掩，
乡愁笼我心上。

译人语

余光中曾云：中文用逗号，是为了文气；英文用逗号，是为了文法。此言大体正确。但也有例外。例如这里的英译：The moon, shining in all splendor, is bathing ....；A glimpse of the moon, wistfully, through ...。两个句子中所使用的前后两个逗号，不仅仅是为了文法，显然婉转了诗的语气。当然，这里的逗号，也可以用破折号代替：一前一后，言语便有了插入语的功能。汉语回译中，"月儿，闪亮"，中间的逗号，正是为了文气；去掉，亦通，但却少了点文气。另外，英译中没有破折号，汉语回译却使用了两个破折号。翻译就是翻译，真正的翻译，乃是变通之道，不仅包括文字的变通，也包括标点的变通。

望月之 101：For Whom the Moon Rises?（明月为谁而升？）

读英文

She **shifted her gaze away from** the group of tourists.
她把目光从这群游客身上移开。

Lighted windows looked gladsome, whiffs of comfortable cookery came abroad upon the air.
透着灯光的窗户让人看了感到高兴，厨房散发出的香味弥漫在空中。

Yet a very little observation shows that **the moon is not standing still**.
但是只稍微观察一会，就知道月亮不是静止不动的。

At a time that seems **to be standing still**.
在一个似乎静止的时间里。

This woman **exercised over him an unaccountable fascination**: he hated her and adored her at the same moment.
眼前这个女人对他来说有种说不清的魔力。他恨她，同时又迷恋她。

The balcony is a park / of the **dreamed cheerfulness**.
阳台是个公园/溢满着梦想的快乐。

Calmness of mind is one of the beautiful jewels of wisdom.
心灵的平静是智慧宝藏中的一朵奇葩。

英文散译

For Whom the Moon Rises?

Light? Hoarfrost? I shift my gaze away from the frosty floor before my bed to the lighted window, without which I catch a glimpse of a brilliant wheel of moon in the high sky. The moon and time seem to be standing still, when the disc is exercising over me an unaccountable fascination — all of a sudden, I find the moon a container of dreamed cheerfulness mixed with a touch of homesickness, which fills my eyes until they are brimming with it. The moon is approachable; calmness of mind is reachable. The moon rises — only for the moongazer.

英文诗译

For Whom the Moon Rises?
Light? Hoarfrost? I shift my gaze
away from the frosty floor before
my bed to the lighted window,
without which I catch a glimpse
of a brilliant wheel of moon in the
high sky. The moon and time seem
to be standing still, when the disc is
exercising over me an unaccountable
fascination — all of a sudden, I
find the moon a container of dreamed
cheerfulness mixed with a touch of
homesickness, which fills my eyes
until they are brimming with it.
The moon is approachable; calmness
of mind is reachable. The moon
rises — only for the moongazer.

回译

明月为谁而升?
光? 霜? 我把目光

从床前如霜的地上
移开，看向光亮之窗：
只见窗外一轮
灿兮兮之明月，
高悬空中。月亮和时间
似乎静滞，冰轮，
对我施展莫名之
魅力——突然之间，我
觉得月亮是个容器，
盈溢着梦中的快乐，
掺兑着几分乡愁，流注
双目，直至盈满。
月亮可及；心灵之
平静，可及。明月
升空——只为观月之人。

译人语

英文译诗标题 *For Whom the Moon Rises?*，源于海明威的小说名字：*For Whom the Bell Tolls?*（《丧钟为谁而鸣？》）汉语回译《明月为谁而升？》，同样借鉴于海明威小说题目的汉译。译诗开头：Light? Hoarfrost?（光？霜？），从李白诗句"床前明月光，疑是地上霜"的行尾汉字捻出，却显得无比巧妙：这床前之光，究竟是月光呢，还是白霜？随后，The moon and time seem to be standing still（月亮和时间似乎静滞），大有意境。深夜之月，不是"月亮走我也走"之月，而是静思默想之月。此句一处，译诗似乎融入了时空观的概念，将夜晚的静谧提升到一个新的高度，凸显诗人在茫茫天地间的渺小，令人想起张若虚《春江花月夜》里的"江天一色无纤尘，皎皎空中孤月轮"，又想起李白《把酒问月》中的"今人不见古时月，今月曾经照古人。"然后，把月亮比作 container（容器），里面装满 dreamed cheerfulness mixed with a touch of homesickness（梦中的快乐，掺兑着几分乡愁），具新诗之质感与分量。

就音韵而言，译诗虽散体出之，不求尾韵，却有"间关莺语花底滑"之感。例如：gaze, away, 元音韵；from, frosty, floor, before, 头韵；window, without, which，头韵；seem，standing，still，头韵；high，sky，尾韵；approachable，reachable，尾韵；moon，moongazer，同异词语，头韵兼元音韵。于是，译诗虽无诗行尾韵而音节自然流畅，或如"大珠小珠落玉盘"，或似"间关莺语花底滑"。译诗最后，The moon rises — only for the moongazer.（明月升空——只为观月之人。）正好回答了诗题之问：*For Whom the Moon Rises?*（《明月为谁而升？》）

望月之 102：Still Night Thoughts（静夜之思）

读英文

When next I awoke, a sickly yellow **light was filtering in on me**.
我再次醒来时，一道暗淡的黄光透进来，照在我身上。

Slowly he followed it with his eyes, winding in wide sweeps among the bleak, bare hills, bleaker and barer and lower-lying than any hills he had yet encountered.
他的目光缓缓地跟随着河流望去。只见它蜿蜒流过一段宽广的河道，河两岸的小山荒芜光秃，比以往见过的任何小山还要荒芜、光秃、低矮。

The **windows** were small, **glazed with little diamond-shaped panes**, and they opened outward, on hinges, like doors.
窗户很小，装着菱形的小窗格，窗上安着铰链，像门一样朝外开。

His talk **was evocative of** the bygone days.
他的谈话令人回忆起往昔的时日。

London is **a kaleidoscopic world**.
伦敦是个万花筒般的世界。

I don't know why I am **in such a reminiscent mood**.
不知为何我这般怀旧。

英文散译

Still Night Thoughts

A still night sees me awake from a sound sleep, when a glittering silvery light, like hoarfrost, is filtering in on me. Slowly, I trace the source of luminosity with my eyes, to the moon without the window which is glazed with little diamond-shaped panes, evocative of the kaleidoscopic world in my long-lost childhood, reducing me into a reminiscent mood.

英文诗译

Still Night Thoughts

A still night sees me
awake from a sound
sleep, when a glittering
silvery light, like hoar-
frost, is filtering in on
me. Slowly, I trace
the source of luminosity
with my eyes, to the
moon without the window
which is glazed with
little diamond-shaped
panes, evocative
of the kaleidoscopic
world in my long-lost
childhood, reducing me
into a reminiscent mood.

回译

静夜之思
静夜，我从酣睡
中醒来，一束

闪烁的银光，如霜，

渗入，照我身上。

慢慢地，我眼睛寻光，

只见窗外，装饰菱形

的格窗之外，一轮

明月——令我想起

我的童年时代，那

万花筒般的世界——

念兹在兹：怀旧，

追忆，那逝去的年代。

译人语

曾读到歌德的一首诗，从德语翻译成英文：*Night Thoughts*，令人想起李白之《静夜思》，前置定语 Still，便成为此英译诗题：*Still Night Thoughts*，回译《静夜思》，其实正好，为了避免"不译之译"，加一"之"字，成为《静夜之思》，亦好。借鉴英文之时，有时可稍微改动。例如：译文中，a glittering silvery light, like hoarfrost, is filtering in on me，借鉴自这个句子：When next I awoke, a sickly yellow light was filtering in on me.（我再次醒来时，一道暗淡的黄光透进来，照在我身上。）显然，借鉴后的译义，添加了 like hoarfrost 这一插入成分，使译文契合原诗之意境，也更具英文之美感。

再如，译文 Slowly, I trace the source of luminosity with my eyes，源自英文句子：Slowly he followed it with his eyes, winding in wide sweeps among the bleak, bare hills, bleaker and barer and lower-lying than any hills he had yet encountered.（他的目光缓缓地跟随着河流望去。只见它蜿蜒流过一段宽广的河道，河两岸的小山荒芜光秃，比以往见过的任何小山还要荒芜、光秃、低矮。）译文只是"拿来"了英文句子中的 slowly, with ... eyes，其它地方都有改动，以适应译文之意、之境。汉语回译的最后："令我想起我的童年时代，那万花筒般的世界——念兹在兹：怀旧，追忆，那逝去的年代"，对应英文：evocative of the kaleidoscopic world in my long-lost childhood, reducing me into a reminiscent mood，有语序调整，有一词多译，手法灵活。整体观之，英文译诗 16 行，汉语回译 12 行。不拘其形，重在译意也。

望月之 103：Tranquil Night Thoughts（静夜，思……）

读英文

Toward daylight of the same morning, Tom Canty **stirred out of a heavy sleep** and opened his eyes in the dark.

同一天，天刚刚放亮时，汤姆·坎蒂从沉睡中醒来，在黑暗中睁开双眼。

About five o'clock Henry VIII. awoke out of an **unrefreshing** nap, and muttered to himself.

大约五点钟，亨利八世从小睡中醒来，仍没解乏，自己咕哝着。

I could see **the faint gleam of light** in the distance.
我能看见远处微弱的灯光。

After a time he **opened his eyes** again, and **gazed vacantly** around **until his glance rested upon** the kneeling Lord Chancellor.

过了一会儿，他又睁开了双眼，神情茫然地环视四周，最后，目光落在了跪着的大法官身上。

In his dream he reached his sordid home all out of breath, but **with eyes dancing with grateful enthusiasm**.

在梦里，他气喘吁吁地回到了自己脏兮兮的家，可眼睛里跳跃着感激的热情。

The King's **face lit up with a fierce joy**.

国王一阵狂喜，容光焕发。

Alack, **how have I longed for this sweet hour**!
哎呀，我是多么盼望这个美好的时刻啊！

The King dropped into inarticulate mumblings, shaking his grey head weakly from time to time, and **gropingly trying to recollect what he had done with the Seal**.

国王开始口齿不清地哼哼，有时微弱地摇摇灰白的头，暗自努力回忆他把御玺放在了什么地方。

He was surprised by **the triviality of** her anxieties.
她对琐碎小事的忧心忡忡使他感到惊讶。

英文散译

Tranquil Night Thoughts

I am stirred out of a heavy, unrefreshing sleep, by a faint gleam of light on the floor before my bed — hoarfrost? I open my eyes, and gaze vacantly around until my glance rests upon the moon without the window, with eyes dancing with grateful enthusiasm, and my face lights up with a fierce joy. How have I longed for this sweet hour! Gropingly, I try to recollect what I have dreamed in my fond dream, when the trivialities of my former domestic life begin to present themselves ....

英文诗译

Tranquil Night Thoughts

I am stirred out of a heavy,
unrefreshing sleep, by a faint
gleam of light on the floor
before my bed — hoarfrost?
I open my eyes, and gaze
vacantly around until my glance
rests upon the moon without
the window, with eyes dancing
with grateful enthusiasm, and

my face lights up with a fierce

joy. How have I longed for this

sweet hour! Gropingly, I try to

recollect what I have dreamed in

my fond dream, when the trivialities

of my former domestic life

begin to present themselves ....

回译

静夜，思……
一束微弱之光，横过
床前地面——我从
沉睡中醒来，心怀
一帘幽梦：白霜？
我睁开双眼，神情
茫然地环视四周；
最后，目光落在窗外
的月亮之上，眼里
闪动着感恩之情，
内心喜悦，面容焕然。
这美好的时刻，乃是
我心之所盼！寻寻觅觅，
我试图回忆梦中所梦；
与此同时，童年家乡
生活的点点滴滴，
在我脑海里浮现……

译人语

译诗标题 *Tranquil Night Thoughts*，与之前的诗题 *Still Night Thoughts* 相仿佛：结构类似，同样精短，只是形容词有所改变。相应的汉语回译，相似却不同：前译《静夜之思》，在李白《静夜思》中加"之"而成；此处诗题，《静夜，思……》，虽然简单，却显得独辟蹊径，有灵思之闪动：在李白诗题《静夜思》里，加一逗号，着一省略号，诗意出矣。

回译中，"心怀一帘幽梦"，措词向雅，主要源于 unrefreshing（不提神的；不使人精神焕发的）一词，此即意味着美梦不足时，突然醒来，没有睡好，意犹未尽。英文译诗中，How have I longed for this sweet hour!直接借鉴自阅读来的英文句子，书上的汉语译文："我是多么盼望这个美好的时刻啊！"在小说或散文中当然可以，但如果照搬这里，恐怕不行：诗意不足。因此，一番思索之后，润色译文如下："这美好的时刻，乃是我心之所盼！"随后的回译中，"寻寻觅觅"，令人读之亲切，对应的英文是 gropingly，若按照"读英文"中相应的译文"暗自努力"，也不太妥帖。"与此同时"，大概对应 when，语气自然而婉转，如此才好。"童年"，对应 former—— 当然无法对应，调整顺应而已；domestic life，若译为"家庭生活"，则离乡思甚远；现用"家乡生活"，虽一字之差，却接近《静夜思》之意。最后，to present themselves，英文大嘉，汉译可用"出现"、"呈现"、"浮现"等词，斟酌后，选用后者。

望月之 104：Dreamy Moonlight & Dreamy Home（梦幻之月光·梦幻之家乡）

读英文

She had just **woken from a deep sleep**.

她刚从熟睡中醒来。

As the afternoon wasted away, the lad, wearied with his troubles, sank gradually into **a tranquil** and healing **slumber**.

下午过去了，这孩子因烦恼而疲乏，渐渐地沉静下来，进入了疗伤的睡梦中。

It startled him disagreeably, and he unmuffled his head to see whence this interruption proceeded.

他被惊醒了，很不高兴，于是探出脑袋，看看哪来的惊扰。

A grim and unsightly picture met his eye.

他看到的是一幅令人厌恶、不堪入目的场景。

Stillness reigns, the torches blink dully, **the time drags heavily**.

四周一片寂静，火炬无精打采地闪烁着，时间拖拉着沉重的脚步一点一滴地流逝。

Hendon contemplated him **lovingly** a while, then said to himself—

亨登慈爱地凝视了他一会儿，然后自言自语说。

But at last the lagging daylight asserts itself, the torches are extinguished, and **a mellow radiance suffuses the great spaces**.

但是，迟来的日光终于宣布了自己的到来。火炬熄灭了，柔美的光线充满了这个伟大的地方。

The mock King's cheeks were flushed with excitement, **his eyes were flashing, his senses swam in a delirium of pleasure**.

假国王的脸颊因兴奋而发红，眼睛闪着光芒，他的感觉沉浸在近乎疯癫的欢乐中。

Wonderfully transported were the people with the loving answers and gestures of their King.

国王深情的回答和举止让人们激动不已。

At first he **pined for** them, **sorrowed for** them, **longed to** see them.

刚开始，他还想念她们，并为之感到悲伤，渴望见到她们。

英文散译

Dreamy Moonlight & Dreamy Home

I wake from a tranquil slumber, when a beam of glittering moonlight startles me agreeably. A sightly and dreamy picture meets my eye: the floor is silvery with frosty stillness which reigns as time drags filmily. Lovingly, I lift my gaze at the moon, whose mellow radiance is suffusing the small space — my eyes are flashing, and my senses are swimming in a pleasure arising from my being wonderfully transported homeward. My home, my sweet home, I pine for you, sorrow for you, long to see you.

英文诗译

Dreamy Moonlight & Dreamy Home

I wake from a tranquil
slumber, when a beam
of glittering moonlight
startles me agreeably.

A sightly and dreamy
picture meets my eye:
the floor is silvery with
frosty stillness which
reigns as time drags
filmily. Lovingly, I lift
my gaze at the moon,
whose mellow radiance
is suffusing the small
space — my eyes are
flashing, and my senses
are swimming in a pleasure
arising from my being wonderfully transported homeward.
My home, my sweet home,
I pine for you, sorrow
for you, long to see you.

回译

梦幻之月光 · 梦幻之家乡

一束闪烁的月光
惊动了我，欣欣然，
我从宁静的熟睡中
醒来。眼前是一副
宜人的梦幻之景：
地上一片银白，
四周寂静如霜；
时间一点一滴地流逝，
柔柔轻轻。深情地，
我抬头注目明月，
柔美的光线充满

小小的空间——
满眼光芒多闪烁，
我的感官沉浸在
欢乐之中——源自
一种奇妙的感觉：
我心，正畅游故国。
我的家，我甜蜜的家，
我想念你，想你
想到我心痛——
我渴望着，能够见到你。

译人语

英文诗题 *Dreamy Moonlight & Dreamy Home*，回译：《梦幻之月光 · 梦幻之家乡》，铢两悉称。译文首句：I wake from a tranquil slumber，借鉴自“读英文”的前两个英文句子，从第一个英文句子中“拿来”wake from，从第二个英文句子中“拿来”tranquil 和 slumber。随后，agreeably，汉语回译“欣欣然”，源于朱自清的散文《春》：“一切都像刚睡醒的样子，欣欣然张开了眼。”然后，time drags filmily，词少而意丰：动词 drag，“拖；拉；缓慢行进”之意，搭配 time，生动形象；filmily，“薄膜地；像软片地”，英文容易意会，汉语却难言传。整句回译：“时间一点一滴地流逝，柔柔轻轻。”只是大意，英文词语的微妙之处，难以尽传。

汉语回译中，英文 my eyes are flashing，对应“满眼光芒多闪烁”，灵感源于五代时期无名氏作品《浣溪沙 · 五两竿头风欲平》中的一个诗行：“满眼风波多闪灼，看山恰似走来迎。”英文表述 my being wonderfully transported homeward，对应“我心，正畅游故国”，源自苏轼《念奴娇 · 赤壁怀古》中的句子：“故国神游，多情应笑我，早生华发。”诗尾的 sorrow for you，其中，sorrow 为动词：“悲伤；惋惜；悔恨”之意，对应汉语“想你想到我心痛”——有一首流畅歌曲，名字就叫《想你想到我心痛》。因此，古诗英译，应该借鉴英文；而英文译诗的汉语回译，若借鉴汉语之经典，同样可以提升译文的质量。

望月之 105：Wishful Thinking in the Depth of Night（深夜痴想）

读英文

About nine, the clouds suddenly break away and **a shaft of sunshine cleaves the mellow atmosphere**, and drifts slowly along the ranks of ladies.

大约九点，云彩突然不见了踪影，一束太阳光穿过柔美的空气，沿着一排一排的夫人、小姐慢慢地漂移。

Yet **through the silence** something throbs, and gleams ...

然而，就是在这种静谧里，有什么东西在砰砰地跳动，在发着光……

Moonlight filters through the window-doors.

月光从长窗透入。

He was beginning to be afraid he had come to the wrong planet, when a coil of gold, the color of the moonlight, **flashed across the sand**.

他开始担心自己来错了地方。这时，他看到一圈金灿灿的东西，月光一样的颜色，在沙地上闪闪发光。

The song of the pulley was still in my ears, and I could **see the sunlight shimmer in the still trembling water**.

辘轳歌还在我的耳边回响，我能看见阳光在晃动的水面上闪耀。

All features of the noble building are distinct now, but **soft and dreamy**, for the sun is lightly veiled with clouds.

现在，这座高贵的建筑的所有特点都清晰可见，只是显得柔和而梦幻，因为太阳微微被云层遮掩。

He stood gazing at the fair young face **like one transfixed.**

他好像被钉在了那里，呆呆地看着这张美丽年轻的脸。

After a long while, the old man, **who was still gazing, — yet not seeing, his mind having settled into a dreamy abstraction,** — observed, on a sudden, that the boy's eyes were open! wide open and staring!—staring up in frozen horror at the knife.

过了好一会儿，老人还在凝视着，但什么都没看见，他的精神正处于游离状态。突然，他发现那男孩双眼睁着！他双眼圆睁，目不转睛地盯着上面的刀子，吓呆了。

A faint tinge appeared for a moment in the lady's cheek, and **she dropped her eyes to the floor.**

这时，女士的脸颊了微微泛红，低下眼睛低看着地板。

The next moment Sir Miles's **thoughts had gone back to** the recent episode. **So absorbed was he in his musings**, that when the King presently handed him the paper which he had been writing, he received it and pocketed it without being conscious of the act.

迈尔斯的思绪马上又回到了眼前的状况。他陷入了深深的沉思，以至于不一会儿国王递给他自己写的信时，他接了过来放进兜里，却没有意识到自己这一系列的动作。

Let us go backward a few hours, and **place ourselves in** Westminster Abbey, at four o'clock in the morning of this memorable Coronation Day.

让我们倒回几个钟头，回到难忘的加冕日那天凌晨四点的威斯敏斯特教堂。

英文散译

Wishful Thinking in the Depth of Night

A shaft of moonshine, through the silence, cleaves the mellow atmosphere, filters through the window, and flashes, frost-like, across the floor before my bed, shimmering, soft and dreamy, in my eyes. I sit up gazing at the moon like one transfixed — for a long while, I am still gazing, yet not seeing, my mind having settled into a dreamy abstraction. Then I drop my eyes to the floor, my thoughts going back to my childhood as I place myself in my old hometown, long lost in the passage of time, absorbed in my musings ….

英文诗译

Wishful Thinking in the Depth of Night
A shaft of moonshine, through
the silence, cleaves the mellow
atmosphere, filters through
the window, and flashes,
frost-like, across the floor
before my bed, shimmering,
soft and dreamy, in my eyes.
I sit up gazing at the moon
like one transfixed — for
a long while, I am still gazing,
yet not seeing, my mind having
settled into a dreamy abstraction.
Then I drop my eyes to the floor,
my thoughts going back to my
childhood as I place myself
in my old hometown, long
lost in the passage of time,
absorbed in my musings ….

回译

深夜痴想
一束月光，在静谧
之中，穿过柔美的
空气，从窗户透入
——如银似霜，闪过
床前的地面，在我眼里

微光轻烁：柔和、梦幻。
我坐起观月，如钉毡上
——过了好一会儿，
我仍然凝视着，却
凝视无睹；我的思想，
处于游离状态。然后，
我垂下眼睛，看着地板，
思想回到童年时代，
想象着自己回到了
遥远的故乡——那早已
遗失在时间的长河之中
的故乡。于是，我陷入
到深深的沉思之中……

译人语

英文译诗的标题：*Wishful Thinking in the Depth of Night*，一次，偶然读到美国作家 Lang Leav 的一首英文诗：*Wishful Thinking*，就想起《静夜思》的英译来。汉语回译《深夜痴想》，发挥了汉语四字结构的优势。译诗在对英文的借鉴中，常有插入成分，从而使得英文句子更加地道、有致。例如，A shaft of moonshine, through the silence, cleaves the mellow atmosphere，其中，through the silence 源自"读英文"第二个句子，其余来自第一个句子；随后的 frost-like，以及 soft and dreamy 等，都是插入成分。

汉语回译中，"如钉毡上"，灵感来自成语"如坐针毡"。"我仍然凝视着，却凝视无睹"，对应英文 I am still gazing, yet not seeing，细品，也算不错的译文。英文译诗的最后六行：Then I drop my eyes to the floor, my thoughts going back to my childhood as I place myself in my old hometown, long lost in the passage of time, absorbed in my musings ....对应中文："然后，我垂下眼睛，看着地板，思想回到童年时代，想象着自己回到了遥远的故乡——那早已遗失在时间的长河之中的故乡。于是，我陷入到深深的沉思之中……"比读，可知英文平淡，汉语却稍显浓彩。

望月之 106：Home Thoughts in the Dead of Night（夜深人静思乡时）

读英文

Home Thoughts from Abroad
异域乡思；海外乡愁

I crept out of bed **in the dead of night** and sneaked downstairs.
深夜我悄悄地从床上爬起来，蹑手蹑脚地下了楼。

He can see **a glimmer of light** through the curtain.
他能透过窗帘看到一丝微光。

He **stole into** the room.
他潜入房间。

Hendon replied **with a solemnity which chilled the air about him**.
亨登的回答带着严肃的语气，使得周围的空气都冷却了。

A window that gave permission to the moon as it watched us from afar.
一扇窗户，让月光进来，月亮在远方看着我们。

He **was soon absorbed in thought**.
他很快陷入了沉思。

The lady walked slowly, **with her head bowed and her eyes fixed upon the floor**.
女士走得很慢，头低着，眼睛盯着地板。

And why do **thoughts arise** in your hearts?

为什么心里起疑念呢？

英文散译

Home Thoughts in the Dead of Night

A glimmer of light steals, frostlike, into the room, onto the floor before my bed, with a solemnity which chills the air about me. I direct my gaze to the window, which gives permission to the moon as it watches me from afar, and I am soon absorbed in thought, with my head bowed and my eyes fixed upon the floor, home thoughts arising ….

英文诗译

Home Thoughts in the Dead of Night

A glimmer of light steals,

frostlike, into the room,

onto the floor before

my bed, with a solemnity

which chills the air about

me. I direct my gaze

to the window, which

gives permission to the

moon as it watches me

from afar, and I am soon

absorbed in thought, with

my head bowed and my

eyes fixed upon the floor,

home thoughts arising ….

回译

夜深人静思乡时

一丝微光，如霜，

潜入房间，落在

我床前的地面上；
一股肃穆之气，
周围的空气冷却
凝霜。我目光向窗，
便见一轮明月——
明月正观望着我，
从远远的远方。
我马上陷入沉思，
低头，目视地板，
乡愁四起……

译人语

英文译诗，由两个句子组成：有插入，如 frostlike；有平行结构，如 into the room 和 onto the floor before my bed；有介词短语，如 with a solemnity which chills the air about me；有定语从句，如 which gives permission to the moon as it watches me from afar，有伴随状语，如 home thoughts arising...。抑扬顿挫，平缓相间；措词讲究，句子耐读——都是借鉴好的英文之所获。整体观之，英文译诗 14 行，汉语回译 12 行。意足，即可；若太过讲究行行对应，则必犯"形式主义至上"的错误。

望月之 107：The Moon as Inner Compass（月亮：心里的罗盘）

读英义

A deep hush pervaded the Abbey.
大教堂里一片深沉的安静。

Only the birds, **awakened by** the sound, flew past them and disappeared among the branches, while some frightened deer fled precipitately before them.
只有被叫声惊醒的鸟儿从他们眼前飞过，又消失在茂密的枝叶中，还有几只受惊的小鹿，慌慌张张地从他们面前飞奔而过。

He awoke in his right mind, lying on his back on a rocky ledge.
他醒来时，头脑清醒，仰卧在一块岩石上。

"You'll be late," she said, under the impression that **he was still stupid with sleep.**
"你要迟到了。"母亲说道，她以为他还睡得稀里糊涂的。

The sun **was shining bright and warm**.
太阳发出明亮而温暖的光芒。

His nerves had become blunted, numb, while **his mind was filled with weird visions and delicious dreams.**
他的神经已经变得迟钝、麻木，但他的脑海里却充满了不可思议的幻想和美好的梦境。

One **loses by** pride **and gains by** modesty.

满招损，谦受益。

He is rich that has few wants.

寡欲者富。

A holiday gives one a chance to look backward and forward, to reset oneself by **an inner compass**.

假期使你有机会回顾与前瞻，用心中的罗盘重新定好自己的方位。

英文散译

The Moon as Inner Compass

A deep hush pervades the room, when I am awakened, not in my right mind, by a beam of light splashing like hoarfrost aground, still stupid with sleep. I lift my gaze, through the window, toward the moon which is shining bright and cold — lying back, my mind is filled with beautiful visions and delicious dreams of my native land. One loses by the burden of life and gains by the bright moon — he is rich that has the moon as his inner compass.

英文诗译

The Moon as Inner Compass

A deep hush pervades
the room, when I am
awakened, not in my right
mind, by a beam of light
splashing like hoarfrost
aground, still stupid with
sleep. I lift my gaze,
through the window,
toward the moon which
is shining bright and cold
— lying back, my mind is
filled with beautiful visions

and delicious dreams of
my native land. One loses
by the burden of life and
gains by the bright moon —
he is rich that has the moon
as his inner compass.

回译

月亮：心里的罗盘
房间里一片深沉
的宁静，一束光，
在地面闪烁，如霜
— 我被惊醒：
头脑稀里糊涂，
半梦半醒。我举目
— 穿窗 —— 看向
明晃晃冷飕飕的
月亮；然后，躺回
床上，脑海里充满
美丽的幻想和美好
的梦境，关于我的
故乡。生活的重担，
使人难堪；明月之
柔光，慰藉我怀。
只要心怀明月，把她
视为心里的罗盘，
就会内心充盈、丰满。

译人语

英文译诗的标题：*The Moon as Inner Compass*，提炼自译诗的最后两行：
he is rich that has the moon as his inner compass，如此，正好。汉语回译，如愣

是译成《作为内心罗盘的月亮》，则效果差矣。稍事琢磨，译为《月亮：心里的罗盘》，初具诗意。英文句子：He awoke in his right mind, lying on his back on a rocky ledge.（他醒来时，头脑清醒，仰卧在一块岩石上。）借鉴后，译文反用：not in my right mind（头脑不太清醒）；随后，still stupid with sleep（睡得稀里糊涂的），进一步补充说明。因此，回译时，将两者合并，译为"头脑稀里糊涂，半梦半醒"。另一个英文句子：The sun was shining bright and warm.（太阳发出明亮而温暖的光芒。）英译 shining bright and cold，把 warm 改成 cold，以符合深夜之月。译诗最后几行：One loses by the burden of life and gains by the bright moon — he is rich that has the moon as his inner compass，从英文好句借鉴而来，表述颇堪玩味，反观汉语回译："生活的重担，使人难堪；明月之柔光，慰藉我怀。只要心怀明月，把她视为心里的罗盘，就会内心充盈、丰满。"似乎只是译出大意，英文措词用语的微妙之处，难以尽传。

望月之 108：Pining Through the Bright, Silvery Quiet（夜思：皎月如银）

读英文

A thread of light emerged from the keyhole.
从钥匙孔透出一线亮光。

As she did so, the moon came out from behind a cloud, and **flooded with its silent silver the little churchyard**, and from a distant copse a nightingale began to sing.
当她完成这一动作后，月亮就从云后出来了，给宁静的小墓园洒满了一片银光，远处的矮树丛里夜莺唱起了歌。

A beautiful light **seemed to illumine her face**.
好像有一道灿烂的光芒照亮了她的脸庞。

He is now **plunged into absorbing reverie.**
他如今正陷入专注的遐想中。

It was moonlight, and he hobbled along **through the bright, silvery quiet, with a vision of life before him that took the form of** a roll of hundred-dollar bills.
皎月如银，他蹒跚着走在这一片静寂中，一边幻想着那一卷百元美钞带给他的美好生活。

Wisdom dawns when names and forms **vanish**.
世间一切名相消失之时，也就是智慧的开端。

英文散译

Pining Through the Bright, Silvery Quiet

A moon emerges from the window, to flood the little room with its silent frost-like silver, seeming to illumine my face. And I am plunged into absorbing reverie, in the dead of night, with a vision of life after me that takes the form of my vanished youth, and my vanished hometown.

英文诗译

Pining Through the Bright, Silvery Quiet

A moon emerges from
the window, to flood
the little room with its
silent frost-like silver,
seeming to illumine my
face. And I am plunged
into absorbing reverie,
in the dead of night,
with a vision of life after
me that takes the form of
my vanished youth, and
my vanished hometown.

回译

夜思：皎月如银
月儿，闪现，自
窗户，灌注小屋，
用其，如霜
之银色：寂静；
似乎照亮，我的
脸庞。我，陷入，
专注的遐想——

夜深，人静，

幻想着：昔日，

生活，如画，如花；

追忆着，逝去的青春，

逝去的——故乡。

译人语

译诗标题：*Pining Through the Bright, Silvery Quiet*，介词 though，有动态感，有"穿过"之含义，非常形象。译诗标题，若直译为汉语，则为："穿越皎月如银的夜晚的思念"，诗化之后，成为《夜思：皎月如银》。"读英文"中的句子：It was moonlight, and he hobbled along through the bright, silvery quiet, with a vision of life before him that took the form of a roll of hundred-dollar bills（皎月如银，他蹒跚着走在这一片静寂中，一边幻想着那一卷百元美钞带给他的美好生活。）其中，a vision of life before him，指未来的生活，但《静夜思》里的思故乡，却是怀念过往的少小时候的生活，因此，介词 before，改成 after 才好：with a vision of life after me that takes the form of my vanished youth, and my vanished hometown。这里，短语 take the form of，也惟妙惟肖，汉译不易言传。另外，整体观之，汉语回译中，多用逗号，以表示时间的延迟与缓慢。文气的逗号，在中文中尤显。

望月之 109：Thoughts of Home in Perfect Stillness（宁静——思乡）

读英文

The night continued clear. **The moon, riding in mid-heaven, diffused her rays on all sides**.

夜色依然明亮。半空中的月亮将光芒洒向四面八方。

Occasionally **the effect of the moonlight on the waters was as though** the boat sailed across a glittering silver field. Little wavelets rippled along the banks. It was enchanting.

偶尔，月光照在水面上，船就像行驶在一片银光闪闪的水域上。微波沿着河岸泛开涟漪。这太迷人了。

The rooms were lofty, **a ripple of sunshine flowed over** the ceilings.

房间很高，一道闪烁不定的阳光在天花板上移动。

The blackness of darkness reigned, **the perfect stillness was interrupted only by** occasional mutterings of distant thunder.

夜色深深，万籁俱静，只有远处偶尔传来的一两声雷声。

The slow days drifted on, and each left behind it a slightly lightened weight of apprehension.

漫长的日子一天天过去了，沉重的恐惧感也一点点减轻了。

Judge Thatcher sent messages of hope and encouragement from the cave, but

they conveyed no real cheer.

撒切尔法官从洞中派人送来些充满希望和鼓励的消息，可这些并不能让大家真正开心起来。

She emptied her mind of all **thoughts of home**.
她打消了想家的所有念头。

These thoughts worked their dim way through Huck's mind, and under the weariness they gave him he fell asleep.

哈克迷迷糊糊地想着这些，弄得十分疲倦，就睡着了。

Huck's face lost its tranquil content, and took a melancholy cast.
哈克脸上的悠然自得立马消失了，一副愁相。

英文散译

Thoughts of Home in Perfect Stillness

The moon, riding in mid-heaven, diffuses her rays on all sides, when their effect in the room is as though ripples of moonshine flow frostily over the bedside floor. The perfect stillness is interrupted only by light from the moon, as the slow minutes and hours drift on. The moongazing conveys a real cheer, when my thoughts of home are working their dim way through my mind, before my face loses its tranquil content and takes a melancholy cast.

英文诗译

Thoughts of Home in Perfect Stillness

The moon, riding in mid-
heaven, diffuses her rays
on all sides, when their effect
in the room is as though
ripples of moonshine flow
frostily over the bedside floor.
The perfect stillness is
interrupted only by light from
the moon, as the slow minutes

and hours drift on. The moongazing
conveys a real cheer, when my
thoughts of home are working
their dim way through my mind,
before my face loses its tranquil
content and takes a melancholy cast.

回译

宁静——思乡
月亮，半空中的月亮，
将光芒洒向四面八方；
月照屋内，似乎一道道
闪烁不定的月光，
清冷如霜，流淌在床前
的地板之上。万籁俱寂，
只有来自月亮的亮光——
一分钟，何其漫长；一小
时，其犹未央。观月，
乃赏心之乐事；此时，
乡思之念，却上心头
——朦朦胧胧，懵懵
懂懂。而我的脸上，
也消了从容，失了
淡定——一副愁相。

译人语

英文译诗标题：*Thoughts of Home in Perfect Stillness*，直译汉语：《完美宁静中的乡思》，不太令人满意，于是，改译为《宁静——思乡》。改变幅度较大，破折号起到了较好的作用。英语译文中，when their effect in the room is …，小词 effect 不可小瞧：词义微妙，却有精微之美。同样，汉语难以言传，认真比读汉语回译，似乎找不出 effect 的译文痕迹。整体而言，英语译文多用水之意象的暗喻，例如：ripples of moonshine flow，drift on 等，都用水做比喻。其实，古诗中常有月光如水之比喻，例如："月光如水水如天"（赵嘏《江楼感旧》），《静夜思》虽然没有如此明示，译文同样可以向水而联想。另外，perfect stillness 和 thoughts of home，这个两个短语都出现在英语译文中，从而呼应诗题 *Thoughts of Home in Perfect Stillness*。

望月之 110：Home-thoughts Revive in the Depth of Night（深夜，乡愁再起）

读英文

How far back can you **trace** your family tree?
你的家谱可以追溯到多少代？

There came over her a nostalgia for the place.
她很眷恋此地。

A strange feeling comes over me.
一种奇怪的感觉支配着我。

I have just visited **the place of my nativity**.
我刚去过我出生的地方。

Many a wayfarer upon the high road which ran by Ferrier's farm felt **long-forgotten thoughts revive in their mind** as they watched her lithe girlish figure tripping through the wheat fields, or met her mounted upon her father's mustang, and managing it with all the ease and grace of a true child of the West.

  不知有多少路人在经过费里尔家农场旁的大道时，瞧见露西那少女的倩影轻盈地穿过麦田，或者碰见她骑着父亲的马，以地道的西部儿女的轻松和优雅驾驭它，见到这样的情景，人们都不禁浮想起那些早已逝去的青春记忆。

英文散译

Home-thoughts Revive in the Depth of Night
The bedside floor is silvery with beams of light glittering like hoarfrost — the

source of which is traced to the moon without the window, and there comes over me a nostalgia for the place of my nativity, and the thoughts, the long-forgotten home-thoughts, revive in my mind.

英文诗译

Home-thoughts Revive in the Depth of Night
The bedside floor is silvery
with beams of light glittering
like hoarfrost — the source
of which is traced to the moon
without the window, and
there comes over me a nostalgia
for the place of my nativity,
and the thoughts, the long-forgotten
home-thoughts, revive in my mind.

回译

深夜，乡愁再起
床前，银白的地上，
一束一束的月光，
闪烁，似霜——
求其源，见窗外
之月，眷恋之情顿生：
那生我养我的地方，
久违的乡思，久违
的乡愁，在我的
心头，被重新唤醒。

译人语

英文诗题 Home-thoughts Revive in the Depth of Night，汉语回译也稍显灵活：《深夜，乡愁再起》，从逗号到语气，都有古语之联想，因而雅致有味。英语译文中，语词常有新颖之处。例如：the place of my nativity（生我养我的地方），一般人不太常用，却是地道之英文。另外，the thoughts, the long-forgotten home-thoughts, revive in my mind，借鉴自英文：long-forgotten thoughts revive in their mind，创译之处，在于 thoughts 的反复：先给出一个简单的 the thoughts，接着补充具体信息：the long-forgotten home-thoughts，然后再续接动词 revive，强调思乡之外，还起到了因插入成分而产生的形断意连的美学效果。

望月之 111：Nostalgia in the Depth of Night（夜半乡愁）

读英文

She tried her best **to poise herself**.

她尽全力使身体保持平衡。

The snow had ceased falling, and the air became **crisp and cold**.

雪已经停了，天气变得极其寒冷。

But **the sad sight moved none to merriment**.

但没人被这令人心酸的场景逗笑。

Gerald stood transfixed, **his soul echoing in horror**.

杰拉德呆立着，心中满是恐惧。

There was silence while one might count ten; the master **was gathering his wrath**.

寂静持续了大约十秒钟，老师越来越生气。

英文散译

Nostalgia in the Depth of Night

The silvery, frosty scene on the bedside floor is the reflection of the moon which is poising itself in the crisp and cold air without the window — this sight moves me to nostalgia, in which my soul is echoing, as silence is gathering in the depth of night.

英文诗译

Nostalgia in the Depth of Night
The silvery, frosty scene
on the bedside floor
is the reflection of
the moon which is
poising itself in the
crisp and cold air
without the window ——
this sight moves me
to nostalgia, in which
my soul is echoing,
as silence is gathering
in the depth of night.

回译

夜半乡愁
床前，地上：
如银，似霜——
源自窗外，
空中之悬月：
空空，清清凉凉。
此生，此夜，
正长好——
引乡愁无限，
心中满是乡思；
值此深更，
值此半夜：
静，愈静。

译人语

英文诗题 *Nostalgia in the Depth of Night*，汉语回译《夜半乡愁》；翻译的

时候，想起小时候学过一篇课文，题目是《夜半鸡叫》，由此而来。文内的回译，如"此生，此夜，正长好"，借鉴自"此生此夜不长好，明月明年何处看。"（苏轼《阳关曲·暮云收尽溢清寒》）；"心中满是乡思"，借鉴自流行歌曲《梦醒时分》中的歌词："你说你犯了不该犯的错，心中满是悔恨。"至于英文译诗，因有英文之借鉴，也常言语清晰可爱。例如 is poising itself in the crisp and cold air，this sight moves me to nostalgia，my soul is echoing，silence is gathering 等，均属当代英文，耐读而富有美感。

望月之 112：Mid-Air Moon in the Mid-Night（**深夜，空中之月**）

读英文

A terrible sheet of lightning burst before their eyes, illuminating the dark day, and the thunder rolled wildly about them.

一道恐怖的闪电在他们眼前一闪，照亮了黑暗的天空，紧接着就是一阵轰轰隆隆的、发疯般的雷鸣。

Pale **rays of light tiptoed** across the waters.

苍白的光轻轻地映在湖面上。

A light fall of snow had obliterated all footmarks; and **a deathly silence pervaded the island**, as if for a space Nature stood still in horror of the recent carnage.

一场小雪遮住了所有的脚印，一片死寂笼罩了整座岛，好像大自然一时让刚才的大屠杀吓到了。

He was thinking of turning back in despair, when **casting his eyes upwards he saw a sight which sent a thrill of pleasure through his heart**.

正打算空手回去的时候，忽然抬头一看，不禁心花怒放。

Outside **all was calm and quiet. The night was fine**, and the stars were twinkling brightly overhead.

门外一片寂静。夜色朗朗，点点繁星在头上闪烁发光。

Everything was fantastically quiet. **In the quiet mid-night, I thought of an array of things**.

而在这寂静的深夜里，我也想起了好多好多的东西。

He seemed to **pine for** his lost youth.

他似乎在怀念他逝去的青春。

英文散译

Mid-Air Moon in the Mid-Night

A silvery sheet of light tiptoes through the window, and falls, like a light fall of frost, onto the floor before my bed, as a deathly silence pervades the room. I cast my eyes upwards, to see a sight which sends a thrill of pleasure through my heart — a moon, a mid-air moon in the calm and quiet mid-night which is so fine. I think of an array of the past things, and I begin to pine for my lost home, my lost youth.

英文诗译

Mid-Air Moon in the Mid-Night

A silvery sheet of light
tiptoes through the window,
and falls, like a light fall
of frost, onto the floor
before my bed, as a deathly
silence pervades the room.
I cast my eyes upwards,
to see a sight which sends
a thrill of pleasure through
my heart — a moon, a mid-air
moon in the calm and quiet
mid-night which is so fine.
I think of an array of the past
things, and I begin to pine for
my lost home, my lost youth.

回译

> 深夜，空中之月
> 一道银色的闪光，
> 轻轻悄悄地，穿
> 窗，如同空里流
> 霜，落在床前的
> 地板之上——一
> 片死寂，笼罩着
> 整个小屋。抬头
> 望：见午夜美景，
> 内心霎时清爽——
> 一轮明月，悬于
> 寂静的空中，恰
> 夜色朗朗。多少
> 往事，涌上心头；
> 我怀念——我的
> 青春，我的故乡。

译人语

英文诗题 *Mid-Air Moon in the Mid-Night*，回译：《深夜，空中之月》，几乎是直译，但却仍感余味。因为逗号的使用——文气的逗号，再次得以验证。英文译诗的开头：A silvery sheet of light tiptoes through the window，用了拟人手法：tiptoe，"用脚尖走"之意。相应的汉译，"穿窗"云云，没有了拟人效果：也只能如此，不可硬译。随后，and falls, like a light fall of frost，这里的两个 fall，前者动词，后者名词，同源词语，效果颇佳。其它地方也不少给人印象深刻之语，如 I cast my eyes upwards，sends a thrill of pleasure through my heart，an array of the past things 等。汉语回译中，仍有典雅汉语之借用。例如："如同空里流霜"，乃是联想到张若虚《春江花月夜》中的"空里流霜不觉飞"，而出之。

望月之 113：The Moon as an Inducer of Nostalgia（乡愁：都是月亮惹的祸）

读英文

In the silence he heard a gentle scratching sound—low, but very distinct in **the quiet of the night**.

万籁俱寂中，他听到一阵轻微的爬抓声——声音虽然很轻，但是在夜深人静的时候，却听得非常清楚。

The weather was clear, and **slightly chilly**.

天气很晴朗，但稍微有点冷。

But **the soft, sweet light of the evening** had waned and gone, and night had absolutely come upon her…

但此时，那柔美的霞光逐渐褪去，茫茫的夜色将她笼罩。

The medicine will **induce** sleep.

这种药会引起睡意。

Diana, by now, **was reduced to her more normal state of** vagueness.

现在，黛安娜再次进入茫然的状态。

Peter breathed in deeply, **savoring the beauty of the night,** and **relishing the thought of happy years** to be spent in Fairacre.

彼得深深呼吸，品味着夜晚之美；想到即将在费雷克斯度过愉快的岁月，心里就美滋滋的。

英文散译

The Moon as an Inducer of Nostalgia

In the silence, the quiet of the room is penetrated by a beam of frostily silvery light, when I wake up to feel slightly chilly. The moon, producer of the soft, sweet light of the deep night, is also a great inducer of nostalgia, and I am reduced to a state of homesickness, savoring the beauty of the night, and relishing the thought of happy years which have been spent in my native land.

英文诗译

The Moon as an Inducer of Nostalgia

In the silence, the quiet

of the room is penetrated

by a beam of frostily silvery

light, when I wake up to feel

slightly chilly. The moon,

producer of the soft, sweet

light of the deep night,

is also a great inducer

of nostalgia, and I am

reduced to a state of

homesickness, savoring

the beauty of the night,

and relishing the thought

of happy years which have

been spent in my native land.

回译

乡愁：都是月亮惹的祸
万籁俱寂中，
屋内之静，
被一束冷霜似

的银光刺穿——
醒来，我感觉微寒。
月亮，深深的柔美
夜色的生产者，
也是乡愁的引子啊——
我不禁思绪飘逸，
品味着夜色之美；
忆起在故乡
度过的那些
幸福的日子，
我的心窝窝里，
就温情溢漾。

译人语

英文诗题 *The Moon as an Inducer of Nostalgia*，若直译：《月亮，乡愁之诱导物》，则不太容易理解，改译为《乡愁：都是月亮惹的祸》，效果好多了，令人想起歌词："我承认都是月亮惹的祸，那样的夜色太美你太温柔"，歌名就叫《都是月亮惹的祸》。"读英文"中，The medicine will induce sleep（这种药会引起睡意），其中，动词 induce，"引起；促使；劝服；引诱"之意。英文译诗中，借鉴此一动词之后，将其改为名词来使用：The moon …a great inducer of nostalgia（月亮，也是乡愁的引子），大佳；再加上 producer 的使用，翻倍其效果。其实，英文里此类-er 词语的应用，构成英文的优势。汉语回译中，同样试图发挥汉语的优势，如"感觉微寒"，"思绪飘逸"，"心窝窝里"，"温情溢漾"等，都是地道汉语，也是汉语四字结构的体现。

望月之 114：Sense and Nonsense in the Depth of Night（深夜：意义与无意义）

读英文

Now little feet tap **at the end of my bed**.
一双双小脚在我的床尾轻轻地走来走去。

"What did you say?" asked M. de Treville, glancing round to see if they were surely alone, and then **fixing his questioning look upon** D'Artagnan.
"你刚才说什么？"德特雷维尔环顾一周，看到没其他人后，又将他询问的目光转向达塔尼昂。

Madame Bonacieux followed him with her eyes, **with that long, fond look** with which a woman accompanies the man whom she feels she loves.
波那瑟夫人目送他离去，那种长久的、深情的目光，就像是一个女子目送自己的爱人一样。

This evening, especially, Aramis **was melancholy and thoughtful**.
今晚，阿拉米显得格外心事重重。

You are talking **complete nonsense**.
你说的全是废话。

Lisa **sensed** that he did not believe her.
莉萨意识到他不相信她。

I **had the sense that** he was worried about something.
我感觉他有心事。

That sounds very **sensible** to me.

我觉得这很合理。

Anger, sadness, & **a deep sense of emptiness** would be a recurring theme & source of frustration.

愤怒，悲伤，深深的空虚感，将是反复出现的主题，也是挫败感的来源。

It's **senseless** to continue any further.

再继续下去，毫无意义。

Life must be **lived forwards** but can only **be understood backwards**.

生活还是要往前过，但只能在回顾中，才能理解。

He only comes here **once in a blue moon**.

他只是偶尔到这儿来一次。

His remarks convicted him of a lack of **sensitivity**.

他的言辞显示了他缺乏敏感性。

英文散译

Sense and Nonsense in the Depth of Night

The silvery light on the floor at the end of my bed is taken as a thin film of frost, before I fix my look — a long, fond one — upon the moon without the window, and I am melancholy and thoughtful. Nonsense, complete nonsense, I sense it in such a strange bed on such a strange floor of such a strange room in such a strange land — I have the sense that it is sensible for me to sense nothing but a deep sense of emptiness: it is senseless to live forwards like this, yet everything can be understood backwards with the passage of time, at least once in a blue moon — when all of a sudden I again catch a glimpse of the moon with sharp sensitivity.

英文诗译

Sense and Nonsense in the Depth of Night

The silvery light on the floor at

the end of my bed is taken as a thin

film of frost, before I fix my look —

a long, fond one — upon the moon

without the window, and I am
melancholy and thoughtful. Nonsense,
complete nonsense, I sense it in such
a strange bed on such a strange floor
of such a strange room in such a
strange land — I have the sense that
it is sensible for me to sense nothing
but a deep sense of emptiness: it is
senseless to live forwards like this,
yet everything can be understood
backwards with the passage of time,
at least once in a blue moon — when
all of a sudden I again catch a glimpse
of the moon with sharp sensitivity.

回译

深夜：意义与无意义
床头的地上，闪烁着
银光，似乎是一层薄霜。
我定睛看——长久、
深情的目光——看着
窗外之月，变得忧沉，
心事重重。无聊，真是
无聊，在这陌生的土地上，
陌生的房间里，陌生的
地板上，陌生的窄床上，
我感到无聊。似乎，这样
合情合理：除了深深的
空虚感，我没有任何感觉
——这样生活，似无甚
意义，而随着时间的流逝，

回顾过往，一切可解——
至少偶尔可解。突然之间，
我再次看见了月亮——
带着独特的敏感性。

译人语

英文译诗中，I fix my look — a long, fond one — upon the moon without the window，前后两个破折号，表示中间是插入成分，带来语言上形断意连的美学效果。另外，两个并列的形容词 long 与 fond，不用 and，却用逗号，其实英文中常见——中国译者会用者似乎不多，英文阅读量少的缘故；还有，one 作为之前 look 的代词，也颇具韵味——英文味。其后，I sense it in such a strange bed on such a strange floor of such a strange room in such a strange land（在这陌生的土地上，陌生的房间里，陌生的地板上，陌生的窄床上，我感到无聊），一口气使用四个 strange（陌生的），强化诗人"独在异乡为异客"之孤独感。

英文译诗中，连用四个 strange 之外，词汇上更为明显的特征，该是 sense 及其派生词的大量使用：sense（名词），sense（动词），nonsense，sensible，senseless，sensitivity 等，个别词语尚有复用。因此，英文译诗的主题，似乎通过这一连串的 sense 词汇，便体现出来。再看诗题：Sense and Nonsense in the Depth of Night，也出现了 sense 与 nonsense，对应之汉语回译：《深夜：意义与无意义》。显然，译诗似乎倾向了点儿哲理思考：Nonsense, complete nonsense（无聊，真是无聊）；甚至，to sense nothing but a deep sense of emptiness（除了深深的空虚感，我没有任何感觉）。这些，"都是月亮惹的祸"；不过，那些过去了的，都将成为美好的回忆。因而诗云：yet everything can be understood backwards with the passage of time（而随着时间的流逝，回顾过往，一切可解）。诗之结尾：all of a sudden I again catch a glimpse of the moon with sharp sensitivity（突然之间，我再次看见了月亮——带着独特的敏感性），似有禅意在其中，令人回而味之。

总之，诗意，往深里译；诗语，借鉴而化用。译文不像译文，译诗不像译诗，倒像是纯正英文之创作，或疑某位英语作家之名作，如此，便是汉诗英译之真正成功。

望月之 115：A Straggler Bathed in Moonlight and Frost（月光霜照独夜人）

读英文

And lo! **through the painted windows came the sunlight streaming upon him**, and the sunbeams wove round him a tissued robe that was fairer than the robe that had been fashioned for his pleasure.

瞧！阳光透过漆窗照在他的身上，光线在他的四周织出一件织锦长袍，比那件专为取悦他而织成的长袍更加精美。

But while he sat inactive **the frost was stealing in on him**, and the quick chilling of his body warned him that he could not delay.

然而，就在他这样一动不动地坐着的时候，严寒偷偷向他袭来；身体骤然打了个寒战，提醒他不能再拖延了。

Her eyes moved gradually out into the velvet dusk.
渐渐地，他的眼睛向外，看着天鹅绒般的暮色。

There comes a smoke from the north, without a **straggler** in the ranks.
有烟从北而来，在他的队伍中没有落伍者。

The last **stragglers** are just finishing the race.
跑在最后面的人刚刚到达终点。

I **bury my face in my hands**.
我用手把脸捂住。

英文散译

A Straggler Bathed in Moonlight and Frost

Through the latticed window comes the moonlight streaming upon me, when I awake to find the bedside floor coated with a thin film of frost, seeming to be stealing in on me. Gradually I move my eyes out into the night sky and, as a straggler, I bury my head in my hands ….

英文诗译

A Straggler Bathed in Moonlight and Frost

Through the latticed
window comes the moon-
light streaming upon me,
when I awake to find
the bedside floor coated
with a thin film of frost,
seeming to be stealing
in on me. Gradually
I move my eyes out
into the night sky and,
as a straggler, I bury
my head in my hands ….

回译

月光霜照独夜人
透过方格之窗，
月光照我身上；
我醒来，只见
床前地面，铺
一层薄薄白霜，
似乎正袭我身
上。渐渐地，

我眼睛向外，
凝望夜空——
作为独夜人，
我双手抱头，
低头不语……

译人语

英文译诗标题 *A Straggler Bathed in Moonlight and Frost*，与 "望月之 58" 的英译标题 *A Straggler in a Moonlit Night* 相似，相应的汉语回译：《月光霜照独夜人》和《月光琅照独夜人》，只有一字之差。这里，"霜照" 之 "霜"，作副词用，似有诗意。译诗中的 straggler，大有深意。"望月之 38" 的英译中，就用到了 straggler；"望月之 58" 英文译诗的标题，即为 *A Straggler in a Moonlit Night*，这里再用，不厌其烦。

英译中，描写月光，…comes the moonlight streaming upon me…，先用一般的抽象动词 come，再用具体动词 streaming，表述细微而妙，若非借鉴英文，译文难以如此。随后，a thin film of frost, seeming to be stealing in on me，头韵明显，节奏轻快；相应的汉译："铺一层薄薄白霜，似乎正袭我身上"——月照我身，霜袭我身：月光如霜来照人，因而标题《月光霜照独夜人》。译诗倒数第五行开始，Gradually I move my eyes out into the night sky and, as a straggler, I bury my head in my hands ….，其中 move，看似简单，若不读英文学习，定不会使用；I，my，eyes，night，sky，押元音韵；move，my，my，my，押头韵；bury，head，hands，押头韵。这些，都保证了译诗明快的节奏。

望月之 116：The Moon & My Childhood Memories（月亮与童年的记忆）

读英文

The crimson **room bloomed with light**.
红色的房间里，光亮如花之盛开。

Moonlight **drips through** the leaves.
月光透过树叶撒在地面。

Pale **rays of light tiptoed** across the waters.
苍白的光轻轻地映在湖面上。

He **rested a curious gaze on** the strange woman.
他好奇地盯着那个怪异的女人看。

You **peer upward**.
你往上看。

He **gazed longingly at** the fat, purple, overripe grapes.
他看着那肥嘟嘟的、熟透了的紫色葡萄，垂涎三尺。

Many past memories crowded in upon his mind.
种种往事一齐涌上他的心头。

英文散译

The Moon & My Childhood Memories

My little room is blooming with rays of light, which are dripping and tiptoeing through the window. I rest a curious gaze on the bedside floor — bright with light? or frost? I peer upward, to gaze longingly at the bright wheel of moon, when many past memories of my childhood are crowding in upon my mind ….

英文诗译

The Moon & My Childhood Memories
My little room is
blooming with rays
of light, which are
dripping and tiptoeing
through the window.
I rest a curious gaze
on the bedside floor
— bright with light?
or frost? I peer upward,
to gaze longingly at
the bright wheel of
moon, when many past
memories of my child-
hood are crowding
in upon my mind ….

回译

月亮与童年的记忆
我小小的卧室
里，一束束
光亮，犹如花
之盛开；光透，
入窗，悄悄
洒落进来。
好奇地，我

凝视着床前
的地面——
光亮？还是白霜？
抬头望，深情地，
我看着天上的
一轮明月，童年
的往事，一齐
涌到我的心上……

译人语

《静夜思》，重在思乡，而乡思之重，重在童年。因此，英文译诗标题 *The Moon & My Childhood Memories*，对应汉语回译《月亮与童年的记忆》。译诗开头：My little room is blooming with rays of light（我小小的卧室里，一束束光亮，犹如花之盛开），可令人想起美丽如花的童年时代。随后，月光与冷霜，形成对比与反差：月光代表着温馨：对于童年往事的回想；冷霜暗示着现实：人生的风霜雨雪，必须勇敢面对。如此，也算是对李白"床前明月光，疑是地上霜"的另类解读了吧。接下来，I peer upward, to gaze longingly at the bright wheel of moon, when many past memories of my childhood are crowding in upon my mind ....（抬头望，深情地，我看着天上的一轮明月，童年的往事，一齐涌到我的心上……）："举头望明月"，明显译出，且详且细；"低头思故乡"中，"低头"未译，因其只是一种艺术符号，表示情绪低落而已，翻译之时，不必当真；"思故乡"，又细化译出："童年的往事，一齐涌到我的心上……"。详略得当，翻译之道。

望月之 117：Fond Memories Dredged up by the Moon（甜美的回忆，月亮勾起）

读英文

They heaped the stacks of hay as high as the straw roof, and in that manner they made a sort of great chamber with four walls of fodder, warm and perfumed, where they should **sleep splendidly**.

他们将一捆捆的干草堆起来，都碰到了茅屋顶，他们就这样替自己安排好了一间四面以干草为墙的宽敞卧室，又温暖又清香，在这里他们一定可以睡得很舒服。

Well, about two in the morning I had sunk into a light sleep when **I was suddenly aroused by** a slight noise.

大约凌晨两点钟的时候，我刚要睡着，突然被一阵轻微的声响弄醒了。

With lips parted, and eyes dim with wonder, he sat idle in his boat and listened, listening till the sea-mists crept round him, and **the wandering moon stained his brown limbs with silver**.

他张着嘴巴，神情黯然，眼里充满疑惑。他呆呆地坐在船上聆听着，一直听到茫茫海雾笼罩在他的四周，而月亮游荡在夜空，银白的月光撒在他那晒黑的四肢上。

The Yankees all **turned their gaze toward her resplendent orb**, kissed their hands, called her by all kinds of endearing names.

所有的美国佬都抬头凝望着这颗灿烂的星球，向她频频飞吻，用各种亲昵的名字呼唤她。

The sun was **high in the sky, blazing down on** us.
太阳高挂在空中，朝我们发出耀眼的光芒。

The sight of it still dredged up sad memories.
眼前的景象还是勾起了 些让人悲伤的回忆。

Then, slowly, **memories of the night thronged into his brain**.
然后，前晚的回忆慢慢地涌进他的大脑。

At these moments I wept bitterly and wished that **peace would revisit my mind** only that I might afford them consolation and happiness.

在这样的时候，我痛苦地哭了，我希望自己的心灵能重新获得平静，只有那样，我才能给他们带来慰藉和幸福。

英文散译

Fond Memories Dredged up by the Moon

I am sleeping splendidly when suddenly aroused by the wandering moon which is staining my limbs with silver — the bedside floor, seemingly, is also silvered with frost which is ethereal; I turn my gaze toward the resplendent orb, high in the sky, blazing down on the good earth — the sight of it dredges up fond memories of my childhood, which are thronging into my brain, as peace revisits my mind.

英文诗译

Fond Memories Dredged up by the Moon

I am sleeping splendidly
when suddenly aroused
by the wandering moon
which is staining my limbs
with silver — the bedside
floor, seemingly, is also
silvered with frost which
is ethereal; I turn my gaze

toward the resplendent orb,

high in the sky, blazing down

on the good earth — the sight

of it dredges up fond memories

of my childhood, which are

thronging into my brain,

as peace revisits my mind.

回译

甜美的回忆，月亮勾起

我正睡得舒舒服服，

突然被弄醒——游荡

的月亮，把银白的

月光，撒在我的四肢

之上。床前的地上，

似乎，也敷了一层

缥缈如银的白霜。

我抬头，凝望着明晃

晃的月球：高悬空中，

朝着大地，发出耀眼

之光——眼前的景象，

勾起了童年时代甜美

的回忆，慢慢地，

涌进我的头脑，而我

的心灵，也重获平静。

译人语

英译诗题 *Fond Memories Dredged up by the Moon*，回译《甜美的回忆，月亮勾起》，令人又想起那首流行歌曲《都是月亮惹的祸》。是的，《静夜思》，就是"月亮惹的祸"。译诗中，sleeping splendidly，双词头韵，若非阅读英文，则想不起来如此搭配；the wandering moon，令人想起电影《流浪地球》：既然

望月之 117: Fond Memories Dredged up by the Moon
（甜美的回忆，月亮勾起）

地球可以流浪，月亮，自然可以流浪了。此处，wandering 的使用，大嘉。若非借助英文阅读，也想不起来这样运用。随后，staining my limbs with silver（把银白的月光，撒在我的四肢之上），其实，动词 stain，乃"弄脏；玷污；着色"之意，如此，大有诗意，极富联想。译文中，两用 silver，先用名词，后用动词，并连通 frost，将"银"与"霜"联系起来：其实，两者都源于月色，且都 ethereal（缥缈若幻），从而凸显了意境之美。译文倒数第四行中，dredge，意为"疏浚，挖掘；采捞"；dredge up，表示"挖掘；提起往事，回忆起"；于是，dredges up fond memories of my childhood 的表述，颇耐回味。译文最后，thronging into my brain 和 peace revisits my mind 等，也属新颖之措词用语。

望月之 118: Flight of Thoughts in the Depth of Night（深夜，联翩之浮想）

读英文

The dull, gray **light** of morning **is stealing into** the cell, **and falls upon** the form of the attendant turnkey.

早晨呆滞、灰暗的光悄悄地照进牢房来，照在那个陪伴他的监狱看守身上。

A long time he waited, when, with thirst unslaked, he crept back to his horse, rode slowly across **the sun-washed clearing**, and passed into the shelter of the woods beyond.

他等了很久，还是非常口渴，然后他又爬上马，慢慢地穿过阳光照耀的空地，走进了远处树林的阴凉里。

"Hello! How's things up Dawson-way?" queried the foremost, **passing his eye over** Donald and Davy **and settling it upon** the Kid.

"你好！道森的情况怎么样呀？"走在最前面的人询问道。他瞥了一眼唐纳德和戴维，最后把目光定在基德身上。

To the south, just clearing the bleak Henderson Divide, **poised the cold-disked sun**.

一轮冰冷的、圆盘状的太阳悬在正南方，就在那荒凉的亨德森分水岭旁。

Shake off these fatal humors; **the eyes of the world are upon** thee.

摆脱这些阴郁的心情吧，世人的眼睛都在看着您。

My mind is very much engaged with him at present.

我现在满脑子都是他。

The moment he arrived at **this place of his dreams** he began fishing, and fished till nightfall.

一来到这个令他魂牵梦绕的地方，他就开始钓鱼，直到夜幕降临为止。

英文散译

Flight of Thoughts in the Depth of Night

The light of the moon is stealing into the room, and falls upon the bed-side floor which, moon-washed, is frostily silvery. I pass my eye over the window and settle it upon the moon in the high night sky, cold-disked, poising in mid-air — my eyes are upon the moon, and my mind is very much engaged with my hometown, the place of my dreams ….

英文诗译

Flight of Thoughts in the Depth of Night
The light of the moon is
stealing into the room, and
falls upon the bed-side floor
which, moon-washed, is
frostily silvery. I pass my eye
over the window and settle it
upon the moon in the high night
sky, cold-disked, poising in
mid-air — my eyes are upon
the moon, and my mind is very
much engaged with my hometown, the place of my dreams ….

回译

深夜，联翩之浮想
月光，悄悄地，溜进
卧室，照在床前的地上：

地面如洗，冷若银霜。
我瞥眼看窗，然后，
目光定格在月亮之上
——高高的夜空中的
月亮：悬在半空，一轮
冰冷的、圆盘状的月亮。
我的眼睛，看着月亮；
我的脑子，满满的，
都是我的故乡，令我
魂牵梦绕的地方……

译人语

英文译诗标题 *Flight of Thoughts in the Depth of Night*，相应之汉语回译《深夜，联翩之浮想》，似乎更佳。由成语"浮想联翩"，创造性使用，变成"联翩之浮想"，诗意顿生。译诗中，moon-washed（地面如洗），乃是造词，由英文之 the sun-washed clearing 改造而来，令人想起张若虚《春江花月夜》中的诗行："玉户帘中卷不去，捣衣砧上拂还来。"随后，frostily silvery（冷若银霜），将"霜"、"银"并置，凸出李白"地上霜"之意象。

I pass my eye over the window and settle it upon the moon in the high night sky, cold-disked, poising in mid-air（我瞥眼看窗，然后，目光定格在月亮之上——高高的夜空中的月亮：悬在半空，一轮冰冷的、圆盘状的月亮），译文既有借鉴也有创造，尤其是月亮的补充表语: cold-disked, poising in mid-air, 改写自英文 poised the cold-disked sun，不失机巧。之后，my eyes are upon the moon, and my mind is very much engaged with my hometown, the place of my dreams ....（我的眼睛，看着月亮；我的脑子，满满的，都是我的故乡，令我魂牵梦绕的地方……），将三个独立的互不相干的句子，摘其关键词，糅合在一起，却又巧结妙合，天衣无缝。同时，my eyes（我的眼睛）与 my mind（我的脑子），令人想起"身在曹营心在汉"的成语典故，别有其妙。另外，英译中，eye 与 eyes，单数与复数的并用，均属正确。复数之用，自不待言；单数以表复数，最常见者，无非此一成语: Beauty is in the eye of the beholder（情人眼里出西施）。另如最近读到英国著名作家詹姆斯·乔伊斯（James Joyce）《都柏林人》（Dubliners）中的这个句子: He had an eye like a hawk（他有着鹰隼般的目光）。汉诗英译者，当多读英文，并用心观察。

望月之 119：Traces of the Dream in a Moonlit Night（月光·梦影）

读英文

Long lances of sunlight pierced down through the dense foliage far and near, and a few butterflies came fluttering upon the scene.

阳光像长矛一般，刺穿了浓密的树叶，在大地上留下一个个圆斑。几只蝴蝶扇着翅膀，在这美景中翩翩起舞。

And **the bright sunlight was streaming into the room**, and from the trees of the garden and pleasance the birds were singing.

灿烂的阳光洒满了房间，从花园和庭院里传来了树上鸟儿的歌声。

It had been snowing since noon; a little fine snow, that covered the branches as with frozen moss, and **spread a silvery covering over** the dead leaves in the ditches, and covered the roads with a white, yielding carpet, and made still more intense the boundless silence of this ocean of trees.

午后就开始不停地下雪；纤细的小雪花洒在树枝上，结成一层苔藓般的冰花，为沟里的枯叶披上一层银色的被子，也在道路上铺了一张又白又软的地毯，使这片本就无限寂静的林海更加浓厚深沉了。

As the reader proceeded, it was quite apparent that it was a hopeless case, and the little man, with his mouth open and **his eyes fixed upon his face**, looked on with an expression of bewilderment and perplexity irresistibly ludicrous.

从那个人接下来读的内容看，很显然，这个案件没有希望。那个小个子男人张大了嘴，眼珠一动不动地看着朗读者的脸，露出茫然失措的神情，极其滑稽。

The sun came out in full splendor and the sea became as calm as a lake.

初升的太阳光芒四射；大海平静得像湖一样。

While lolling on the grass I **summoned up the dusky recollections of my boyhood respecting this place**, and repeated them like **the imperfectly remembered traces of a dream**, for the entertainment of my companions.

我懒懒地坐在草地上，回想童年关于这个地方的许多朦胧记忆，像记不清楚的梦的片段一样，重复讲给同伴听，就当作消遣。

英文散译

Traces of the Dream in a Moonlit Night

Long lances of moonlight pierce down through the window, streaming into the bedroom, to spread a silvery covering over the frosty floor before my bed. My eyes fix upon the moon without the window, which comes out in full splendor, and the dusky recollections of my childhood respecting my hometown are summoned up, like the imperfectly remembered traces of the dream where I am freshly awakened.

英文诗译

Traces of the Dream in a Moonlit Night

Long lances of moon-
light pierce down through
the window, streaming
into the bedroom, to spread
a silvery covering over
the frosty floor before my
bed. My eyes fix upon
the moon without the window,
which comes out in full
splendor, and the dusky
recollections of my childhood
respecting my hometown
are summoned up, like

the imperfectly remembered

traces of the dream where

I am freshly awakened.

回译

月光·梦影

月光，长矛一般，

刺穿窗户，洒满

卧室，给我床前

的地上，敷上一层

银霜。我盯着窗外

之月，月亮升空，

光芒四射。此情，

此景，唤起我，

童年故乡的朦胧

记忆，恰似依稀

模糊之梦影——

从中，我刚刚醒来。

译人语

英文诗题 *Traces of the Dream in a Moonlit Night*，借鉴了"读英文"中最后一个英文句子中的 traces of a dream，在诗题中，将不定冠词改为定冠词，大意等于"梦影"，描写若虚若幻之梦。诗题的汉语回译，没有直译，而是发挥汉语——包括标点——的优势，将其译为《月光·梦影》，似有诗意。英文译诗两个句子，稍长；汉语回译三个句子，显短。借鉴之后，英文有耐读之处，尤其 the dusky recollections of my childhood respecting my hometown are summoned up, like the imperfectly remembered traces of the dream where I am freshly awakened.（此情，此景，唤起我，童年故乡的朦胧之梦影——从中，我刚刚醒来。）多有借鉴，偶尔改写。另外，英文译诗 16 行，汉语回译 12 行，不拘其形，重在传神。

望月之 120：Moonlight and My Childhood Moon（月光与童年的月亮）

读英文

Moonlight was streaming into the room, and it was bright with a vague and shifty radiance.

月光照进屋内，闪耀着粼粼光辉。

Above all, color **is lent to** this picture by the presence of women.

女人的出现尤其使这幅图画的颜色更为鲜明。

She **gazed with longing eyes on** the sullen, surging waters that lay between her and liberty.

她用渴望的眼神盯着汹涌的河水，如果能够过河，她就自由了。

It was now about noon, and **every thing seemed sunk into repose**, like the bandit that lay sleeping before me.

现在正值晌午，万物都处于沉寂中，就像在我面前睡着的强盗一样。

I was struck with a profound veneration at the sight of Brutus, and **could easily discover** the most consummate virtue, the greatest intrepidity and firmness of mind, the truest love of his country, and general benevolence for mankind, **in every lineament of his countenance**.

我一见到布鲁特斯就觉得肃然起敬，从他脸上的每一点都可以很容易地看出他至高无上的品德，坚定、大无畏的胸怀，最真诚的爱国心以及对人类的热爱。

He **bowed his head in prayer**, and the priests in their stiff copes crept away from the altar.

他叩头祈祷，那些神父们身着僵硬的法袍，悄悄地走下了圣坛。

英文散译

Moonlight and My Childhood Moon

Moonlight is streaming into the bedroom, and it is bright with a vague and shifty radiance, which lends a thin film of seeming frost to the floor before my bed. I gaze with longing eyes on the moon without the window, feeling that every thing seems sunk into repose — I am struck with a profound veneration at the sight of the moon, and can easily discover the charm itself in every thread of light. Which is suggestive of my childhood moon, and I bow my head in homesickness.

英文诗译

Moonlight and My Childhood Moon

Moonlight is streaming
into the bedroom, and
it is bright with a vague
and shifty radiance,
which lends a thin film
of seeming frost to the
floor before my bed.
I gaze with longing
eyes on the moon
without the window,
feeling that every thing
seems sunk into repose
— I am struck with a
profound veneration at
the sight of the moon,
and can easily discover

the charm itself in every
thread of light. Which is
suggestive of my child-
hood moon, and I bow
my head in homesickness.

回译

> 月光与童年的月亮
> 月光流入卧室，
> 发出梦幻莫测
> 之粼粼光芒，
> 给我床前地面，
> 敷上一层薄薄
> 白霜。我盯着
> 窗外的月亮，
> 眼神充满着渴望，
> 感觉万物沉寂——
> 我见月，而肃然
> 起敬；从每条
> 光线中，都可
> 轻易感受到月之
> 魅力。眼前之景，
> 令我想起童年
> 的月亮，于是
> 我低头，陷入
> 乡思，开始思乡……

译人语

《静夜思》，其实由月光，而思乡，童年的故乡；由异乡之月，而想到故乡之月，也就是童年之月，因有诗题 *Moonlight and My Childhood Moon*（《月光与童年的月亮》）。译文 a vague and shifty radiance 中，shifty 为"变化的；诡诈的；机智的"之意，在"望月之 5"的第一个英文句子中，也出现过：She smiled, looking dreamily out on the shifty landscape.（她脸露微笑，用一种梦幻似的目光看着那变化莫测的景色。）因此，结合具体语境，把 a vague and shifty radiance 回译为"梦幻莫测之粼粼光芒"。接下来，动词 lend，也可妙用：非"借给"之意，而是"给……增加；增添（特色）"。还有，gaze with longing eyes on，every thing seems sunk into repose，I am struck with a profound veneration，the charm itself in every thread of light，I bow my head in homesickness 等，因借鉴英文，显得醇厚而有余味。唯有一处，值得注意：Which is suggestive of ….，用在句号之后，并首字母大写，显得奇怪：which 引导的从句，一般都是字母小写，紧随逗号之后。不过，跟在句号之后，并首字母大写如此者，在多年的英文阅读中，也偶尔见过几次。例如：

The grown-ups told me to forget about drawing elephants inside boa constrictors and to concentrate instead on geography, history, arithmetic and grammar. Which is why, at the age of six, ….

在 Which is why 之前，凸显的句号，而且，which 作为关系代词，明显是指之前句子的陈述。大概因为之前的句子太长，如果再不断句，继续使用逗号的话，句子就太过冗长，因此才破格：在不该使用句号的情况下，却使用了句号。再如下面这个英汉对照的句子：

Forty years had rolled by, long and rapid, dreary as a day of sadness and as similar as the hours of a sleepless night. Forty years of which nothing remained, not even a memory, not even a misfortune, since the death of his parents. Nothing.

四十年过去了，漫长而迅速，生活枯燥得就像一个个愁苦的白昼和失眠的漫漫长夜。四十年来，他什么也没留下，连一点回忆也没有，自从他的父母逝世以后，甚至一点不幸也没有。什么都没有。

其中，Forty years of which，只是在 which 之前添加了介词短语，性质却跟 which 引导的从句，完全类似的。这种现象，英文当中本不常见，在汉译英中更是少见。但，却是正确而地道的英文表达。

最后，综合观之，英文译诗共 21 行，汉语回译却 18 行。不拘泥于诗行之对应，只求诗情诗意之忠实传达。自由体或散体译诗，本色如此。

望月之 121：The Powerful Effect of the Midnight Moon（午夜之月：魅不可挡）

读英文

A light was shining in one of the attic windows.

阁楼的窗户里透出一丝光线来。

The meagre **daylight peered in through the grated windows**, and showed him the gaunt figures of the weavers bending over their cases.

微弱的日光透过格栅窗照进阁楼，他看到了织布工伏在织布机上的憔悴身影。

In truth, for the instant she was veiled to him, and what he saw was the wide **sunwashed** spaces of the West, where men and women were bigger than the rotten denizens, as he had encountered them, of the thrice rotten cities of the East.

他没有回答。尽管他的眼睛盯着她，却是一片茫然。顷刻间，她的真面目展现在他的面前。他看到了阳光沐浴下广阔的西部空地，那里的男人和女人都比他在这个堕落太多的东部城市里遇见的居民要大度、亲切。

And **his eyes hungrily bent upon** the finished craft.

一双眼睛贪婪地盯在那条已经完工的船上。

The sun **is shining in all its splendid beauty**.

太阳发出灿烂的光芒。

The noon-tide stillness that reigned over these mountains, the vast landscape below, gleaming with distant towns and dotted with various habitations and signs of life, **yet all so silent, had a powerful effect upon my mind**.

中午时分，群山之间，万物寂静。下面是辽阔的平原，远处的城镇若隐若现，间或有各式各样的住宅，显露出生活的迹象，但一切都那么安静，我被眼前这景色深深触动了。

Silence reigned everywhere.

万籁俱寂。

A vague feeling of uneasiness began to steal over me.

一阵模糊的不安，渐渐涌上心头。

英文散译

The Powerful Effect of the Midnight Moon

A light is peering in through the grated window, when I awake to find the floor moonwashed: frostily silvery. My eyes hungrily bent upon the moon without the window, which, shining in all its splendid beauty through the midnight-tide stillness that reigns everywhere, has a powerful effect upon my mind — a vague feeling of homesickness begins to steal over me....

英文诗译

The Powerful Effect of the Midnight Moon

A light is peering in

through the grated window,

when I awake to find

the floor moonwashed:

frostily silvery. My eyes

hungrily bent upon the

moon without the window,

which, shining in all its

splendid beauty through

the midnight-tide stillness

that reigns everywhere,

has a powerful effect
upon my mind — a vague
feeling of homesickness
begins to steal over me….

回译

午夜之月：魅不可挡
一束光，透过
格栅窗，照进
卧室，我醒来，
发现床前地面，
沐浴在月光之中：
如银似霜。我的
眼睛，贪婪地
盯在窗外的月亮
之上——她正
散发灿烂的光芒，
穿透午夜的万籁
俱寂，深深触动
我的思想———一阵
隐隐约约的乡愁，
悄然涌上心头……

译人语

英文译诗标题 *The Powerful Effect of the Midnight Moon*，乃从译诗之中提炼而出：首先暗含月亮的 moonwashed，然后明示月亮的 the moon without the window，再从 midnight-tide stillness 中，提炼出定语 midnight，成为标题中的 the Midnight Moon；随后的译文中，a powerful effect upon my mind，改写为 the powerful effect of，再与 the Midnight Moon 组合。如此，诗题与诗文产生勾连，效果较好。

英文译诗开头：A light is peering in through the grated window，从"读英

文"前两个句子借鉴而来：a light 源于第一个句子；peer in through the grated window，则改写自第二个句子。随后，moonwashed，显为造词，灵感源自"读英文"第三个句子中的 sunwashed（阳光沐浴的）；虽然只是一个单词，译诗却不少出彩。

随后的译文中，shining in all its splendid beauty through the midnight-tide stillness that reigns everywhere，根据英文句子中的 the noon-tide stillness，改写出 the midnight-tide stillness，续接的 that reigns everywhere，借鉴自下一个英文句子：Silence reigned everywhere（万籁俱寂）。另外，介词 through 的使用，也生动传神，平时阅读积累所致。

望月之 122：Tender Memories Through the Profound Stillness of the Night（细腻而美好的回忆，穿过夜之宁静）

读英文

Try not to let your mind **wander**.
尽量别让你的思想开小差。

Her gaze wandered on beyond the Diogenes' lanterns into the open space.
她的目光越过第欧根尼灯笼花游移着，看到了那片开阔地。

He too **gazed at the pale disc of the moon**, now nearly veiled, and seemed to meditate.
他也凝视着几乎被遮住了的月亮那苍白的圆盘，似乎陷入了沉思。

In the profound stillness of the woodland they could distinguish the current rippling along the rocky shore, and the distant murmuring and roaring of Hell Gate.
林地里一片沉寂，他们能听出水流在岩岸泛起涟漪的声音，还有远处地狱门水道的潺潺声和咆哮声。

And read the names of distant places on the time-bills **with indescribable longings**?
我盯着列车时刻表上所列出的遥远的地名，心中充满了无法描述的憧憬。

He rolled over on his back and shut his eyes, **striving to construct a mental**

picture of the harbor as he had seen it in daytime.

他翻身躺在水面上，闭着眼睛，努力在脑海中构建一幅白天看到的港口的画面。

We, whom the country enchants, **keep tender memories of** certain springs, certain woods, certain pools, certain hills seen very often which have stirred us like joyful events.

我们这些迷恋乡村的人，对于经常见到的某处泉水、树林、池塘和山丘都保留了细腻美好的回忆，它们曾经像喜事一样触动着我们。

英文散译

Tender Memories Through the Profound Stillness of the Night

The bedroom is flooded with glittering light, which seems to coat the floor with an ethereal film of frost. My eyes wander without the window, to gaze at the silvery disc of the moon through the profound stillness of the night with indescribable longings, striving to construct a mental picture of the home as I have seen it in my childhood, of which I still keep tender memories....

英文诗译

Tender Memories Through the Profound Stillness of the Night

The bedroom is flooded
with glittering light,
which seems to coat
the floor with an ethereal
film of frost. My eyes
wander without the window,
to gaze at the silvery disc
of the moon through the
profound stillness of the
night with indescribable
longings, striving to construct
a mental picture of the home

as I have seen it in my child-

hood, of which I still

keep tender memories....

回译

细腻而美好的回忆，穿过夜之宁静

卧室被闪烁之光

淹没，地面似乎

镀上了一层缥缈

的薄霜。我目光

游弋窗外，穿过

夜之宁静，凝望着

月亮那银色的

圆盘，心中

充满难以描述

的憧憬——努力

在脑海中构建

一幅童年时代

的家乡的画面，

这细腻而美好

的回忆……

译人语

英文诗题 *Tender Memories Through the Profound Stillness of the Night*，摘录自译诗，首先出现在第八、九行的 through the profound stillness of the night，然后出现在诗尾的 tender memories，将两个短语倒置，成为诗题。汉语回译《细腻而美好的回忆，穿过夜之宁静》，同样，诗行中首先出现"穿过夜之宁静"（第五、六行），然后出现"细腻而美好的回忆"（诗尾）。英文译诗注意题文呼应，汉语回译，也应该注意，才能产生较好的效果。

"读英文"第二个句子中的 In the profound stillness of the woodland，介词 in，表示静态，改为 through，则译文有动态效果：through the profound stillness of the night。 "望月之 121"中，也有介词 through 的妙用：shining in all its splendid beauty through the midnight-tide stillness that reigns everywhere。

　　译诗最后，striving to construct a mental picture of the home as I have seen it in my childhood, of which I still keep tender memories....，将两个英文句子改造之后，合并一起，做到无缝连接，流畅达意。其中，as I have seen it 的表述方式，看似简单，却令人涵咏。贾平凹的散文《我读何海霞》，刘士聪英译为：*He Haixia, as I Read Him*，多年前读到，竟然没太理解译者的用心。此处之英文，又一证也。

望月之 123：The Moon Begets Homesickness （见月思乡）

读英文

Positive thoughts **beget** positive results.
积极向上的思维，可以产生积极的结果。

I was glad, then, to find that he was my neighbor, and gladder still when, **in the dead of the night**, I heard a whisper close to my ear and found that he had managed to cut an opening in the board which separated us.
我发现他跟我是邻居，非常欢喜，一个夜深人静的晚上，我突然听到几句细语声，回头一看，原来是他设法在囚室隔板上挖了一个洞，这更使我喜不自胜。

He had not exactly lost it; he had climbed **in the dead of night** to the top of the wardrobe and hidden it there.
他并不是真的弄丢了那个瓶子，深夜时分，他爬上柜子顶部，把它藏在那里了。

Jim scarcely **glanced at** them.
吉姆几乎都没看一眼。

Unable to speak, **her eyes were riveted on** the door of the cottage, which she had just opened.
她说不出话来，眼睛盯着她刚刚打开的村舍的门。

As **the sun began to steal in upon the boys, drowsiness came over them** and they went out on the sandbar and lay down to sleep.

　　不知不觉中，太阳已经升起来了。温暖的阳光照在孩子们的身上，把他们弄得昏昏欲睡，最后他们干脆走出林子，躺在沙滩上睡起觉来。

英文散译

The Moon Begets Homesickness

　　In the dead of night my room is alive with beams of light, glittering and playing about my bed, which awakes me from a fond dream. I glance at the bedside floor, which is frostily silvery, and my eyes are riveted on the moon without the window, which is stealing in upon me, as homesickness comes over me ….

英文诗译

The Moon Begets Homesickness

In the dead of night
my room is alive
with beams of light,
glittering and playing
about my bed, which
awakes me from a
fond dream. I glance
at the bedside floor,
which is frostily silvery,
and my eyes are riveted
on the moon without
the window, which is
stealing in upon me,
as homesickness
comes over me ….

回译

　　见月思乡
　　夜深人静的

晚上，屋子
里一束束的
光，闪烁，
照我床上，
把我从梦中
惊醒。我看着
地面，银白
如冷霜，然后，
我的眼睛盯着
窗外的月亮
——月光照在
我的身上，
乡愁，也
袭我心上……

译人语

英文诗题 *The Moon Begets Homesickness*, 若直译, 则是:《月亮引起乡思》, 不够诗意。因此意译为《见月思乡》, 稍好。译文中, In the dead of night my room is alive with beams of light, 一个 dead, 一个 alive, 反义对比, 形成夜晚之静与月光之动的反差。随后, 英文 a fond dream, 汉语回译, 未译"美梦", 只用一个"梦"字, 节奏使然: 梦或美梦, 无关大雅。译诗最后: which is stealing in upon me, as homesickness comes over me ...., 两个短语, 形象生动, 回译汉语:"月光照在我的身上, 乡愁, 也袭我心上……", 通过"身上"与"心上", 形成同源词语, 产生对比与回还之美。

望月之 124：The Bright Moon Is Symbolic of Nostalgia（明月有情寄乡思）

读英文

They opened a gate of wrought ivory, and **I found myself in** a watered garden of seven terraces.

他们打开一道精致的象牙门，我发现自己来到了一个有七个看台的水上花园里。

And on the morning of the seventh day **I lifted up my eyes**, and lo! the city lay at my feet, for it is in a valley.

到了第七天，我抬头望去，看哪！城市就横躺在我的脚下，因为它就位于山谷中。

Gregor then turned **to look out the window at** the dull weather. Drops of rain could be heard hitting the pane, which made him feel quite sad.

随后，格雷戈尔转向窗外看了看阴沉沉的天气。雨滴击打着窗玻璃，这种声音让他感到非常忧伤。

The music **absorbed** young people.

这音乐使年轻人着迷。

She thought just the opposite; **the sight of the bare walls saddened her right**

to her heart.

她的看法恰恰相反。看到光秃秃的墙壁，一阵悲伤就会直袭她的心脏。

英文散译

The Bright Moon Is Symbolic of Nostalgia

Awake from a fond dream, I find myself in a strange room, whose floor is frostily silvery — with light? or the moon? I lift up my eyes, as a wanderer, to look out the window at the moon, which absorbs me immediately. The sight of the bright moon saddens me right to my heart, since it is symbolic of poignant nostalgia.

英文诗译

The Bright Moon Is Symbolic of Nostalgia

Awake from a fond dream,
I find myself in a strange
room, whose floor is
frostily silvery — with
light? or the moon? I lift up
my eyes, as a wanderer,
to look out the window at
the moon, which absorbs me
immediately. The sight of
the bright moon saddens me
right to my heart, since it is
symbolic of poignant nostalgia.

回译

明月有情寄乡思
梦中醒来，我发现
自己置身一个陌生
的房间，地面霜冷
如银——光乎？月乎？
我抬眼，作为天地

宇宙间的一个匆匆
过客，看向窗外
之月：立刻使我
着迷。看到一轮
明月，一阵悲伤
直袭我心——明月
有情，寄千里乡思。

译人语

英文译诗标题 *The Bright Moon Is Symbolic of Nostalgia*，与诗歌最后：it is symbolic of poignant nostalgia，几乎吻合，只是 it 代替了 the bright moon，并在 nostalgia 之前，添加了 poignant 一词；相应的汉语回译："明月有情，寄千里乡思"，与诗题回译《明月有情寄乡思》相比，也添加了逗号和"千里"，以增强其意。

英文译诗中，whose floor is frostily silvery — with light? or the moon? 其中介词 with，非常巧妙，构成 be adj. with 的短语，with 之后，一般表示形容词所描述的状态的原因。汉语回译："地面霜冷如银——光乎？月乎？"意即：地面像冷霜一样银亮，因为光线呢？还是因为月亮呢？只说光线，不一定是月光；而提到月亮，却指的是月亮之光。

随后，独立成分 as a wanderer，英文里暗含沧桑，汉译"天地宇宙间的一个匆匆过客"，虽然繁琐，却正达其意。另外，译文中 a strange room（一个陌生的房间），更烘托了人之作为世间过客的悲怆感。

望月之 125：Deep Thought in a Deep Night（在深夜，我深思）

读英文

The sun **was already high** and **shed a flood of light on** the Bois de Boulogne.

太阳已升得老高，并在布洛涅森林上面投下一层光浪。

She **sent a questing glance across** the tall grass and in and out among the orchard trees.

她的目光扫过在果园内外高高的草丛，似乎在寻找什么。

But Donald **had fixed his gaze** up river, and now his voice rang out, vibrant with fear.

然而唐纳德凝视着河流，突然声音颤抖，其中夹杂着恐惧，大声喊道。

Imber's **head drooped** once more, and his eyes went dull, as though a film rose up and covered them from the world.

英勃尔的头又垂下去，他的双眼变得模糊，好像生了一层薄膜，看不见周围的世界。

While each of the party **was absorbed in reflections** so different, the sledge flew fast over the vast carpet of snow.

当每个人都专注地想着截然不同的心事时，雪橇正快速地飞越广袤无垠的雪地。

Accordingly, he determined to have vengeance, and **remained till daylight in**

an attitude of deep thought.

　　于是他决心报复，一直深思到天明。

英文散译

Deep Thought in a Deep Night

The moon is already high and sheds a flood of light, through the window, into the bedroom, onto the floor, which is frostily silvery. I send a questing glance through the window, before fixing my gaze at the moon. Then, head drooped, I am absorbed in reflections about my childhood and hometown…. Accordingly, I remain till daylight replaces moonlight, in an attitude of deep thought.

英文诗译

Deep Thought in a Deep Night

The moon is already high
and sheds a flood of light,
through the window, into
the bedroom, onto the floor,
which is frostily silvery.
I send a questing glance
through the window, before
fixing my gaze at the moon.
Then, head drooped, I
am absorbed in reflections
about my childhood and
hometown…. Accordingly,
I remain till daylight
replaces moonlight, in
an attitude of deep thought.

回译

　　在深夜，我深思
　　月亮，升得老高，

投下一层光浪
——穿窗，入室，
着地：银冷
如霜。我探求
的目光，扫过
窗户，凝视
空中的月亮。
然后，垂头，
专注地回想，
我的童年，
我的家乡……。
于是，在深夜，
我深思——
月光淡，日光亮。

译人语

英文诗题 *Deep Thought in a Deep Night*，回译原为《深夜，深思》，可谓汉英匹配。后来，汉语回译，诗内用了"在深夜，我深思"之语，才把诗题也改成《在深夜，我深思》，以便产生题文互联之效果。英文诗内，through，into，onto，三个介词并用，均含动态，效果显著，凸出了动态之美。汉语回译，先用一破折号，然后："穿窗，入室，着地"，三个简短的动宾词语，描述动作的轻快与连贯。随后，捻出冒号，用"银冷如霜"的四字汉语，来描述卧室地面之貌。第六行中的 a questing glance（探求的目光），从英文借鉴而来，却巧妙地译出了"疑是地上霜"中"疑"之情态。诗歌最后，Accordingly, I remain till daylight replaces moonlight, in an attitude of deep thought，英文句散，却耐回味；汉语回译："于是，在深夜，我深思——月光淡，日光亮。"显为骈偶之句。各美其美，美美与共。

望月之 126：Silent Night: My Mind Wanders Away（静夜：思绪飘逸）

读英文

His mind wanders whenever he attends a meeting.
他一开会思想就开小差。

But his head was not clear and **his mind wandered away to** the glare and rattle of the public-house.
但是他的脑袋不清楚，思绪则又飘向了酒馆的灯光和叮叮当当的碰撞声。

He could hear nothing: **the night was perfectly silent**. He listened again: perfectly silent. He felt that he was alone.
他什么都听不到：夜出奇地安静。他又听了听：出奇地安静。他感到自己是孤身一人。

Gabriel's **eyes**, irritated by the **floor**, which **glittered with** beeswax under the heavy chandelier, **wandered to** the wall above the piano.
加布里埃尔的眼睛厌倦了那在笨重的枝形吊灯下闪闪发光的打过蜂蜡的地板，于是目光就游移到了钢琴上方的那面墙上。

There is **a splash of** paint on the white wall.
白墙上溅上了一片油漆。

Then he began to roll the tobacco again **meditatively** and after a moment's thought decided to lick the paper.

随后他又开始若有所思地卷起了烟叶，片刻的沉思之后才决定舔湿那张卷烟纸。

The less hilly shores of Loch Katrine westward extended like a picture **framed** between Ben An and Ben Venue.

卡特琳湖山丘较少的湖岸向西延伸，就像一幅镶嵌在本·安和本·凡纽之间的图画。

英文散译

Silent Night: My Mind Wanders Away

A perfectly silent night: the bedside floor is glittering with a splash of whiteness — from frost? or from moonlight? My eyes wander, meditatively, to the window, which is framing a bright wheel of moon, as my mind wanders away, away to my remote hometown ….

英文诗译

Silent Night: My Mind Wanders Away

A perfectly silent
night: the bedside
floor is glittering
with a splash of
whiteness — from
frost? or from
moonlight? My eyes
wander, meditatively,
to the window, which
is framing a bright
wheel of moon, as
my mind wanders
away, away to my
remote hometown ….

回译

静夜：思绪飘逸

宁静之夜，

床前地上，

银闪着一片

白光：冷霜？

还是月光？

沉思中，我

的目光飘向

窗户：窗含

清空一轮月。

随之，我思绪

飘逸，飘到

遥遥远远

袅袅娜娜

的故乡……

译人语

英译诗题 Silent Night: My Mind Wanders Away，读来似感流畅，细看，因前四个单词 Silent，Night，My，Mind 均含同一双元音；Wanders 与 Away，因后者第一个音节轻读，便有头韵之效果。译诗最后，as my mind wanders away, away to my remote hometown ....，重复副词 away，再与介词 to 搭配，呼应了诗题，强化了诗意。诗题汉语回译《静夜：思绪飘逸》，包含李白《静夜思》三字经典："思"为关键，扩展开来，成为"思绪飘逸"。李白的诗歌风格，名言"飘逸"，这里，诗题的回译中，终于用到了"飘逸"二字。

另外，wander 在诗尾反复之外，诗中还有一用：My eyes wander, meditatively, to the window....；主语却是 eyes，不同于之前的主语 mind。译诗中另一亮点，该是动词 frame 的使用：framing a bright wheel of moon（窗户框住了一轮明月），令人想起杜甫《绝句》中的"窗含西岭千秋雪"，相关的英译，有译者采纳 frame 一词，正好。这里，英译的汉语回译："窗含清空一轮月"，显然改自"窗含西岭千秋雪"。回译中，"银闪着"，"银"字，名词用作动词，便有新意生出。"遥遥远远袅袅娜娜"，对应英文一词 remote：浓与淡，各适其所；繁与简，各得其当；秾与朴，各自贴切。译英文如英文，译中文如中文，这才是翻译的正道。

望月之 127：The Depth of Night & the Back of My Mind（深夜·深思）

读英文

A ghastly **light from** the street lamp **lay in a long shaft from one window to the door**.

从街上照进来的一束灰蒙蒙的光线，长长地从一个窗口一直斜射到门口。

The **blinds** would be drawn down and Aunt Kate would be sitting beside him, crying and blowing her nose and telling him how Julia had died.

百叶窗会放下来，凯特姨妈会坐在他的身旁，边哭边擤鼻子并跟他讲朱莉娅是怎么死的。

She **looked away** from him **along the shaft of light towards the window in silence**.

她默默地把目光从他身上移开，顺着那束光线朝窗边望去。

The child asked, **with wondering eyes**.

小女孩张大好奇的眼睛问。

He stood still in the gloom of the hall, trying to catch the air that the voice was singing and **gazing up at** his wife.

他一动不动地站在昏暗的客厅里，一边努力辨识着那声音正在吟唱的调子，一边抬头凝视着妻子。

Then he looked **thoughtfully** before him and said in a calmer tone.

然后他若有所思地看着前方，用一种比较平静的语调说道。

A dull anger **began to gather again at the back of his mind** and the dull fires of his lust began to glow angrily in his veins.

一股隐隐的怒火开始在他的内心深处再次聚集，隐现的欲望之火开始在他的血脉中愤怒地燃烧起来。

英文散译

The Depth of Night & the Back of My Mind

The depth of night sees a bright light from the blinds lying in a long beam to the bed-side floor, which is frostily silvery. I look away, with wondering eyes, along the shaft of light towards the window in silence, to find in the night sky a bright wheel of moon, at which I am gazing up thoughtfully, when homesickness begins to gather at the back of my mind ….

英文诗译

The Depth of Night & the Back of My Mind
The depth of night
sees a bright light
from the blinds lying
in a long beam to
the bed-side floor,
which is frostily
silvery. I look away,
with wondering eyes,
along the shaft of light
towards the window
in silence, to find
in the night sky
a bright wheel of
moon, at which I am
gazing up thoughtfully,

when homesickness

begins to gather at

the back of my mind ….

回译

深夜·深思

深夜，一束

亮光，自百叶

窗，流曳长长

—— 泄到我

床前的地上：

如银，似霜。

我把目光移开，

从地上，顺着

亮光，睁大

好奇的眼睛，

看向窗，静静

悄悄——只见

夜空中，一轮

明月正闪亮。

我若有深思，

凝视着月亮；

乡愁，渐生渐浓，

凝聚在我心上……

译人语

英译时，首先考虑如何将《静夜思》翻译成英文散文，并尽量借鉴"读英文"中的英文表述，以提升译文的品质。整首诗译完之后，才考虑标题的英译。反复阅读译诗，一方面试图百尺竿头更进一步，另一方面，从中寻找或提炼合适的题目。阅读中，突然发现，译诗开头 The depth of night，与译诗结尾 the back of my mind，正好形成对比：夜深人静之时，辗转发侧，不能入眠，正是思乡的时候了啊。于是，诗题顿生：*The Depth of Night & the Back of My Mind*，汉语回译：《深夜·深思》，两个"深"字，一个圆点，汉语诗题亦具诗意。

　　译诗中，为了避免重复，先用 beam 代替了英文句子中的 shaft，随后，才用 shaft 一词。插入语的使用，如 with wondering eyes；语序的倒置，如 at which I am gazing up，源于正常语序：gazing up at；关系副词 when 的添加使用，都体现了译者的创新。借鉴并创新之后，才有好的英文句子和段落：译诗由两个句子组成，一短一长，符合英文起伏跌宕、交错缠绵之态。从英文散译到英文诗译，是个诗歌分行的过程，有时也颇费思量，努力使其走向当代新诗。所谓经典咏流传，就古诗英译而言，也该是中国古诗在英语世界的当代化。汉语回译，则尽量忠于英诗之形、之音、之意。

望月之 128：The Dead of Night & the Wheel of Moon（夜之死寂·月之光华）

读英文

He watched sleepily the flakes, silver and dark, falling obliquely against the lamplight.

他睡意朦胧地注视着那些雪片，银白而暗淡，斜斜地落在路灯上。

His eyes moved to the chair over which she had thrown some of her clothes.

他的目光转移到了她在上面扔了一些衣服的那把椅子。

She turned away from the mirror slowly and **walked along the shaft of light** towards him.

她从镜子旁慢慢转过身来，沿着那束光线朝他走来。

She stopped, choking with sobs, and, **overcome by emotion**, flung herself face downward on the bed, sobbing in the quilt.

她停下来，哽咽地抽泣起来，然后再也控制不住感情，一下子脸朝下地扑到床上，在被子里哭泣起来。

His imagination had so abstracted him that his name was called twice before he answered.

他陶醉于自己的想象当中，叫他名字两次，他才应答。

He had not exactly lost it; he had climbed **in the dead of night** to the top of the wardrobe and hidden it there.

他并不是真的弄丢了那个瓶子，深夜时分，他爬上柜子顶部，把它藏在那里了。

As he stood in the darkness outside the church **these memories came back with the poignancy of vanished things**.

他站在教堂外面的黑地里，这些回忆兜上心头，象已经消失的物件一般的痛切。

英文散译

The Dead of Night & the Wheel of Moon

I watch sleepily the floor before my bed, silver and bright, suggestive of hoarfrost. My eyes move, along the shaft of light, from the floor to the window, out of which I find a bright wheel of moon, and I am overcome by emotion. My imagination has abstracted me, in the dead of night, as the memories come back with the poignancy of vanished things, of my vanished hometown.

英文诗译

The Dead of Night & the Wheel of Moon

I watch sleepily the floor
before my bed, silver and
bright, suggestive of hoarfrost. My eyes move,
along the shaft of light,
from the floor to the window,
out of which I find a bright
wheel of moon, and I am
overcome by emotion.
My imagination has
abstracted me, in the dead
of night, as the memories
come back with the poignancy
of vanished things,

of my vanished hometown.

回译

夜之死寂·月之光华
睡意朦胧地，我
注视着床前地面：
银白而明亮，令人
想起地上之霜。我
目光移动，沿着
那束光，从地面
到窗上，透视一轮
明月，亮晃晃：我
情不自己。陶醉
于遐想之中，在
这深夜时分，一些
回忆兜上心头，像
那流失的东西，像
我消逝的故乡：
怎一个痛字了得！

译人语

英文诗题 *The Dead of Night & the Wheel of Moon*，在译诗中有呼应：分别出现 in the dead of night 和 a bright wheel of moon；汉语回译《夜之死寂·月之光华》，虽然也有诗意，却在译诗中找不到明显的反复，英文之对应回译，分别是"在这深夜时分"和"一轮明月"。如果不变，将"在这深夜时分"和"一轮明月"作为诗题，显然太过散淡。因此，根据诗的内容，提炼出"夜之死寂"和"月之光华"，平行对称，终于稍感满意。

英文译诗中，along the shaft of light（沿着那束光），my imagination has abstracted me（陶醉于遐想之中），the memories come back with the poignancy of vanished things, of my vanished hometown（一些回忆兜上心头，像那流失的东西，像我消逝的故乡：怎一个痛字了得！）因借鉴英文而表达形象生动，描写

惟妙惟肖。回译:"亮晃晃","兜上心头"等,即便在汉语创作中,也算新鲜造语;"怎一个痛字了得",乃是名言套路:"怎一个愁字了得"(李清照《声声慢》),从而感觉亲切。无论从英文译入中文,还是从中文译入英文,都需要发挥译入语的优势,译文或译诗才能取得良好的阅读效果。

望月之 129：Deep Night Brooding （深夜，深思）

读英文

Birds were twittering in the ivy and the sunny web of the curtain **was shimmering along the floor**.

鸟儿在长春藤中欢唱，窗帘后面射进来的阳光，在地板上闪耀。

There are some pictures of women wearing **filmy** nightgowns.

有一些女性照片，她们穿着朦胧的睡衣。

She **raised her head from her arms** and dried her eyes with the back of her hand like a child.

她从臂弯里抬起头，像一个孩子似的用手背擦干眼睛。

A dull, yellow light brooded over the houses and the river; and the sky seemed to be descending.

一种黯然昏黄的光线笼罩着房屋和河流；天空似乎要坠下来的样子。

It's no use **brooding over** one's past mistakes.

老是抱着过去的错误，是没用的。

You seem to **brood over things**.

你好像有什么事，闷在心里。

英文散译

Deep Night Brooding

A beam of light is shimmering along the floor, which looks filmy and frosty. I raise my head from the floor, to find a moon without the window, which is brooding over the great earth, when I begin to brood over things in the past, things of my hometown ....

英文诗译

Deep Night Brooding
A beam of light
is shimmering along
the floor, which looks
filmy and frosty.
I raise my head
from the floor,
to find a moon
without the window,
which is brooding
over the great earth,
when I begin
to brood over
things in the past,
things of my
hometown ....

回译

深夜，深思
一束光，
沿着地板
闪耀，朦胧
如霜。从
地上，我
抬头，看
见窗外的

月亮——月
光正笼罩
大地，在沉
思默想；而
我，也开始
想自己的心
事，想自己
的家乡……

译人语

首先译出散体英文，再琢磨英文诗题：诗中反复短语 brood over，为"忧思；沉思"之意，恰吻合《静夜思》之"思"，因此，抽出动词 brood，变作名词 brooding，再前置 deep night（深夜），成为诗题：*Deep Night Brooding*。回译《深夜，深思》，复用"深"字，凸显思念之深；添加逗号，延缓思念之节奏。

英文译诗中，介词 along 很好：形象地描绘出月照屋内的动态情形；回译用"沿着"，恰好。随后，filmy and frosty 非常好，不仅惟妙惟肖，而且与之前的 floor，形成三词头韵；之后，又发现另外三词头韵：from，floor，find；四词头韵：without，window，which，when；以及 things 的反复，都带来很好的音韵效果。

望月之 130：The Moon Is the Homesickness of Wanderer （月亮引旅人乡思）

读英文

There is a grim look about the houses, **a suggestion of** a jail about those high garden walls.

房子看上去阴森森的，花园四周的高墙使人联想到监狱。

For some time he lay without movement, **the genial sunshine pouring upon him and saturating his miserable body with its warmth**.

他一动不动地躺了好一阵子。温暖的阳光洒在他身上，让那饱受磨难的身体沐浴在阳光的暖意中。

If you had **magic power** for one day, what would you do?

如果你拥有一天的魔法，你会做什么呢？

During the day **a glimpse into the garden is easily obtained through** a wicket to which a bell is attached.

白天的时候，人们可以透过边门轻而易举地瞥见园中的景色。

The sun was **shining bright** and warm.

太阳发出明亮而温暖的光芒。

A mantle of ivy conceals the bricks and attracts the eyes of passers-by **to an effect** which is picturesque in Paris.

常春藤密密麻麻地遮住了砖块，吸引着路人的眼球。这幅景象在巴黎是一道很独特的风景。

An effect where a portion of a background scene is replaced by a new video.
一种背景场景的一部分被一个新的图像替代的效果。

I used to be much convinced and admire him for that he could describe **the miseries in life** so wittily.
我曾经深以为然，并且佩服他把人生的可悲境遇，表述得如此轻松俏皮。

He did not answer and **for a while she allowed her thoughts to wander**.
他没有回答。而她任由自己的思绪自由驰骋一会儿。

Happiness is the poetry of woman, as the toilette is her tinsel.
香水让女人散发魅力，幸福让女人充满诗意。

英文散译

The Moon Is the Homesickness of Wanderer

There is an illusory look, when I awake from a fond dream I am aware of it, about the room: the light is pouring upon me and saturating my body with its magic power. A glimpse of the moon is easily obtained through the window, shining bright, to an effect where the bedroom floor seems to be filmily coated with silvery frost, a suggestion of the miseries in life. For a great while I allow my thoughts to wander — the moon is the homesickness of wanderer, as the icy frost is his transformer.

英文诗译

The Moon Is the Homesickness of Wanderer
There is an illusory look,
when I awake from a fond
dream I am aware of it,
about the room: the light
is pouring upon me and
saturating my body with
its magic power. A glimpse
of the moon is easily obtained

through the window, shining
bright, to an effect where
the bedroom floor seems to be
filmily coated with silvery frost,
a suggestion of the miseries
in life. For a great while I allow
my thoughts to wander —
the moon is the homesickness
of wanderer, as the icy
frost is his transformer.

回译

月亮引旅人乡思
房间看来如梦，
似幻，我从梦中
醒来，感到了
这种梦幻：银
光洒在我身上，
沐浴在光的魔力
之中。透过窗户，
月亮，轻而易举，
一瞥而见：闪照
朗朗——卧室
地面，似乎着了
一层薄薄的冷霜，
暗示人生之艰难。
沉浸良久，我
放飞自己的思想
——月亮引旅人
乡思，冷霜
令游子坚强。

译人语

英文诗题：*The Moon Is the Homesickness of Wanderer*，呼应译诗的最后：the moon is the homesickness of wanderer, as the icy frost is his transformer，这个句子对中国人来说，不太容易理解，借鉴自"读英文"的最后一个句子，需要反复品味，方可会意其妙。其中，wanderer，令人想起英国诗人华兹华斯的名句：I wandered lonely as a cloud；名词 wanderer，恰对应汉语之"游子"：《静夜思》，写游子思乡，最见其痛。另外，transformer，此词一出，或许带来点儿阅读理解上的障碍，而一旦扫除，令人直感其畅快。查阅各种词典，transformer 之汉语释义，概有"变压器；促使改变的人（或物）；转换器；变形金刚"等；这里，the icy frost is his transformer，如若直译，则为："冰霜乃其改造物"，意即经历了人生的冰霜雨雪，游子才得以百变成钢，变得坚强。诗题回译：《月亮引旅人乡思》，尚可；译诗中，接续"冷霜令游子坚强"，平行，成对偶之美。

译诗中，look 接续 about，却被一个从句隔开，产生了形断音连之美学效果；to an effect，意为"（月照屋内）达到了这样的效果"，但汉语回译却不必译出字面；a suggestion of，又借鉴自"读英文"的第一个句子：一个句子，两处借鉴，却同样巧妙。译文更妙之处，是把冷霜比喻成人生之"艰难苦恨"：英文着一 silvery，汉语用之"银光"，则有通往"繁霜鬓"之意图；杜甫之《登高》，极写人生之萧瑟凄凉，一叹！

望月之 131：The Moon as a Spellbinder（月亮醉我）

读英文

In short, there is no **illusory** grace left to **the poverty that reigns here**.
总而言之，一派贫穷的气息笼罩着这里，无法让人产生优雅的联想。

He caught himself up at the question and **glanced** nervously **round the room**.
他纠结于这个问题，不安地环视着房间。

Her abstracted **gaze rested on** the smoothness of the river.
她那漫不经心的目光，落到了平静的河面上。

Surely a clever and high-spirited young man, whose wit and courage were set off to advantage by a graceful figure and the vigorous kind of beauty that **readily strikes** a woman's **imagination**, need not despair of finding a protectress.
他是个聪明、热情的年轻人，优雅的外表和阳刚的气质更是彰显出了他的智慧和勇敢。这样的人肯定很容易叫女性着迷，根本不愁找不见女性保护人。

His strange appearance **struck terror into their hearts**.
他那奇怪的外貌，使他们大吃一惊。

The spell of a factitious energy **was upon him**; he had beheld the pomp and splendor of the world.
虚假的活力让他着了魔。他已经见识到世界壮观、华丽的一面了。

The final game of the tennis match was a real **spellbinder**.
网球的决赛确实异常精彩。

英文散译

The Moon as a Spellbinder

An illusory beam of light enhances the quietude that reigns in the room; I find the floor filmily frosty. I glance, wonderingly, round the room, until my gaze rests on the moon without the window, which readily strikes my imagination, as it does homesickness into my heart. Immediately, the spell of the moon, as a spellbinder, is upon me.

英文诗译

The Moon as a Spellbinder
An illusory beam
of light enhances
the quietude that reigns
in the room; I find
the floor filmily frosty.
I glance, wonderingly,
round the room, until
my gaze rests on the
moon without the window,
which readily strikes my
imagination, as it does
homesickness into my
heart. Immediately, the
spell of the moon, as a
spellbinder, is upon me.

回译

月亮醉我
一束梦幻之光，
凸显屋内之静；
我发现床前

地面，朦胧

似霜。满心疑惑，

我环顾四周，

直到目光落在

窗外的月亮

之上：引发了

我的乡思，

激发了我的

想象。立马，

月亮之魅，

使我着了魔：

月亮——醉我。

译人语

英文诗题：*The Moon As a Spellbinder*，源于译诗的最后两行：the spell of the moon, as a spellbinder, is upon me，发挥了英文之优势。借鉴的英文句子中，the spell of a factitious energy was upon him，译文借鉴之后，还使用了插入成分：as a spellbinder，调节了语气与节奏。同时，spell 与 spellbinder，有同源修辞格之美学效果。

正如"鸟鸣山更幽"，光照屋更静，尤其在这深更半夜。译诗如此开篇，也算有些创意。接下来，I find the floor filmily frosty，头韵效果明显；汉语回译"我发现床前地面，朦胧似霜"，音韵之美，流失殆尽矣。汉诗英译之时，深感英文无法传达汉语之音；英诗汉译之时，尤其是英文里的头韵，也常常是无可奈何花落去。译诗之明显头韵，还有一处：without the window, which....，汉语同样束"译"无策。另外，wonderingly 前后使用逗号，如同前言之 as a spellbinder 一样，做独立之插入成分；代动词 does 的使用，以及前述之同源修辞格等，都独具英文之特色与优势，很难汉译出色。例如，英文动词 strike，大意"引起（感情、情绪等）；使突然充满（一种强烈的情绪）"；the moon...strikes my imagination, as it does (strikes) homesickness into my heart；相应之汉语回译："引发了我的乡思，激发了我的想象"，调整了语序，措词用语，平淡了不少。再如名词 spellbinder，词典上的解释："能吸引听众的演说家"，其实，英文-er

类词，表达力极强，这里显指具有无比魅力之月亮，因有诗题 *The Moon As a Spellbinder*，回译汉语《月亮醉我》，勉强其意而已。

　　总之，本书中《静夜思》英文译诗，较之汉语回译，整体而言，都是英诗醇厚而多余味，汉译淡薄而显局促。原因：英诗灵活多创意，汉诗忠实常直译。

望月之 132：Midnight Homesickness（午夜乡愁）

读英文

Indian thought **is** not easily **traced to its sources**.
印第安人的心思是难以捉摸的。

An enormous full moon. A moon that demands that you stop and take notice. It's hanging over our pond **like a giant lost polka dot**.

一轮大大的满月，令人停下脚步，注目凝望。月亮悬挂在池塘之上，好像从圆点花纹中走失的一个硕大圆点。

His eyes were glued to the keyhole.
他的眼睛紧贴在钥匙孔上。

The young man took the elder's hand, and **looked at him with something like kindness in his eyes**.

年轻人抓起老人的手，看着他，眼神中带着几分善意。

He felt his great body again aching for the comfort of the public-house.
他感到他那壮硕的身体又急需酒馆的慰藉了。

英文散译

Midnight Homesickness

The bedside floor is bright, seemingly with a thin film of silvery frost, the source of which is traced to the light without the window: an enormous full moon hanging in the air like a giant lost polka dot — to which my eyes are glued, with something like homesickness in my eyes, and I feel my heart aching for my dear home.

英文诗译

Midnight Homesickness

The bedside floor is bright,
seemingly with a thin film
of silvery frost, the source
of which is traced to the light
without the window: an
enormous full moon hanging
in the air like a giant lost
polka dot — to which my
eyes are glued, with something like homesickness in
my eyes, and I feel my heart
aching for my dear home.

回译

午夜乡愁
床前地面明亮，
似乎敷上一层
薄薄的银霜——
源于窗外之光：
一轮巨大的满月，
悬于空中，好像
从圆点花纹中走失
的一个硕大圆点。
我的眼睛紧盯着她，

眼神中带着乡愁，

我感到，我的心啊，

在热切地想家！

译人语

此译之亮点，在于月亮之比喻：like a giant lost polka dot（好像从圆点花纹中走失的一个硕大圆点），出人意表之外。根据网上词典，polka dot 意为"圆点花纹"，当指散布很多圆点的花纹布料；前置定语 giant 和 lost，言其巨大，似乎从布料中走失，想象颇为奇特。

随后之英文，to which my eyes are glued，借鉴自第三个英文句子：His eyes were glued to the keyhole.（他的眼睛紧贴在钥匙孔上）；with something like homesickness in my eyes，借鉴自第四个英文句子：looked at him with something like kindness in his eyes（看着他，眼神中带着几分善意）；I feel my heart aching for my dear home，借鉴自第五个英文句子：He felt his great body again aching for the comfort of the public-house（他感到他那壮硕的身体又急需酒馆的慰藉了）。

望月之 133：Deep Night Thoughts（深夜思）

读英文

He ran his greedy eyes over them, searching for the thinnest ones.
他用那贪婪的眼睛扫视他们，寻找最瘦小的人。

"How lovely," cried Wendy so **longingly** that Mrs. Darling tightened her grip.
"多美好啊。"温迪是如此地羡慕，达林夫人不由得紧紧地抓住她。

After the meal they **felt** rusty, and stiff-jointed, and **a little homesick once more**.
吃罢，他们都觉得浑身酸痛，骨节僵硬，于是又有点想家了。

Her imagination carried her far off, and showed her innumerable dangers.
她的想象将她带到了远处，让她看到无数危险。

And again **his thoughts dwelt on his childhood**, and again it was painful and he tried to banish them and fix his mind on something else.
他的思绪再一次停留在他的童年时代，还是令人痛苦，他竭力地驱赶那些回忆，把思绪放在别的事情上。

英文散译

Deep Night Thoughts

A beam of silvery light, through the window, into the room, coats the floor with a film of hoarfrost. When I run my greedy eyes, longingly, over the moon which is framed by the window, I begin to feel a little homesick. My imagination carries me far off, as my thoughts dwell on my childhood, on my hometown....

英文诗译

Deep Night Thoughts

A beam of silvery light,

through the window,

into the room, coats

the floor with a film

of hoarfrost. When I

run my greedy eyes,

longingly, over the

moon which is framed

by the window, I begin

to feel a little homesick.

My imagination carries

me far off, as my thoughts

dwell on my childhood,

on my hometown....

回译

深夜思

一束银光，

穿窗，入室，

敷地面一层

薄薄的白霜。

透窗，我盯着

一轮明月，

观看，眼睛

贪婪而渴望

————一丝乡愁，

袭心上。我的

想象，把我

带到远方；思绪，

停留在我的童年，

我的故乡⋯⋯

译人语

英译中，through the window, into the room，两个介词引起两个短语，平行对仗；对应之汉语："穿窗，入室"，动宾结构，简洁到位。随后，把 coat 用作动词，"涂上；覆盖；包上"，亦好。I run my greedy eyes, longingly, over....，插入副词，有形断意连之效；另外，在句首着一关系副词 When，把主句变成从句，更符合英文散文之恋。My Imagination carries me far off（我的想象，把我带到远方），言身不由己，表述到位；as my thoughts dwell on my childhood, on my hometown....，接续自然，两个 on 的反复，词虽小，而作用大。

回顾诗题，*Deep Night Thoughts*，文中 thoughts 与之呼应，deep night 未在诗中出现，形成互补。汉语回译《深夜思》，与李白之《静夜思》，只差一字。英译与回译，整体看来，英文主句从句并用，短语插入并生；汉语则是逗号延缓节奏，分号破折传情。语言既然不同，标点亦有差异。

望月之 134：The Midnight Moon Works Me into a Passion（深夜之月，燃我激情）

读英文

The last sunshine **fell with romantic affection upon her glowing face**.

最后一抹阳光，照在她发光的脸上，带着浪漫的深情。

Said Aunt Polly, **her face lighting wistfully**.

波莉姨妈问，脸上一副惆怅的神情。

His face lighted with a happy solution of his thought.

他面露喜色，作出了一个愉快的决定。

My heart looks back to its old home.

我的心呀，念想着故园老家。

But always she shook her head and denied him the freedom **for which he worked himself into a passion**.

而她总是摇摇头，拒绝放开他，尽管他如此疯狂地哀求。

He **is** now **plunged into absorbing reverie**.

他如今正陷入专注的遐想中。

英文散译

The Midnight Moon Works Me into a Passion

The depth of night sees me waking to a beam of glittering light, which falls with romantic affection upon my face which is glowing and lighting wistfully. The frost-bathed floor is dreamily silvery — I look up to find a bright moon as my heart looks back to its old home, for which I work myself into a passion, plunged into absorbing reverie ….

英文诗译

The Midnight Moon Works Me into a Passion
The depth of night
sees me waking to
a beam of glittering
light, which falls
with romantic affection
upon my face which
is glowing and lighting
wistfully. The frost-bathed
floor is dreamily silvery
— I look up to find a
bright moon as my heart
looks back to its old home,
for which I work myself
into a passion, plunged
into absorbing reverie ….

回译

深夜之月，燃我激情
深夜，一束
闪烁之光，照
我脸上，带着
浪漫深情；我
从梦中醒来，
脸上有光，却

也充满惆怅。
如同霜洗的地面，
如梦似银——
抬头望，只见
一轮明月，我的
心呀，开启了对
故园老家的念想。
深夜之月，燃我
激情，引我遐想……

译人语

英文译诗开头：The depth of night sees me waking to a beam of glittering light，其中，waking to 的表达，借鉴自一本英文书名：*Early Spring — An Ecologist and Her Children Wake to a Warming World*，作者是 Amy Seidl。

如果比较英文译诗开头的句子及其汉语回译，可见语序的倒置："一束闪烁之光"，提前了；"照我脸上"，也提前了；"我从梦中醒来"，后置了。另外，"脸上有光，却也充满惆怅"，对应英文 my face which is glowing and lighting wistfully，由并列关系转成了偏正关系。英文最后，for which I work myself into a passion, plunged into absorbing reverie，其中的动词 work 和 plunge 等，形象生动，中文回译难传其妙，"深夜之月，燃我激情，引我遐想"，运用四字结构，勉强译之。

望月之 135：Midnight: Imagination Has Free Play（午夜：想象力肆意挥洒）

读英文

Suddenly, too, he saw **a faint gleam of light** on the second story; it came from M. Vautrin's room.

突然，他又看见三楼有微弱的光线从沃尔特兰先生的房里传出。

The rain **seeped through** the roof.

雨水透过房顶渗透。

Farrington **looked at the company out of his heavy dirty eyes**, smiling and at times drawing forth stray drops of liquor from his moustache with the aid of his lower lip.

法林顿用他那深沉浑浊的眼睛看着这帮朋友，微笑着，时不时地用下唇舔去胡须上残留的酒滴。

He **looked at me in a slow and pondering way**, and shook his head.

他慢慢地、若有所思地望着我，然后摇摇头。

Imagination has free play, and turns their lives into a romance.

他们肆意挥洒着想象力，让生活变得十分浪漫。

Stifled laughter from the ante-chamber **added to his confusion**.

前厅传来了偷笑声，这更是让他不知所措。

英文散译

Midnight: Imagination Has Free Play

Midnight sees a faint gleam of light seeping through the window ── out of my passionate eyes, I look at the moon in a slow and pondering way, when imagination has free play. Then I drop my gaze, at the rimed floor before my bed, which adds to my homesickness.

英文诗译

Midnight: Imagination Has Free Play

Midnight sees a faint
gleam of light seeping
through the window ──
out of my passionate
eyes, I look at the moon
in a slow and pondering
way, when imagination
has free play. Then
I drop my gaze, at
the rimed floor before
my bed, which adds
to my homesickness.

回译

午夜：想象力肆意挥洒
午夜，一束微弱
之光，渗透，
穿窗——目光
热切，缓慢而
若有所思地，
我望着月亮，
想象力肆意

挥洒。然后，

我垂下目光，

看着床前如霜

的地面，乡愁，

更愁其愁。

译人语

英文译诗首句，Midnight sees a faint gleam of light seeping through the window，融合了"读英文"中的前两个句子；out of my passionate eyes，借鉴自第三个英文句子，倒装，并融入第四个句子中的表达: in a slow and pondering way；随后，imagination has free play，从第五个句子中直接拿来；which adds to my homesickness，是对第六个句子借鉴后的改写。另外，Then I drop my gaze，逗号之后，才出来介词 at，表示望月动作的缓慢与时间的延迟；若无此逗号，效果大不相同。

汉语回译中，"目光热切，缓慢而若有所思地"，对英文 passionate eyes 和 in a slow and pondering way 进行了合并。把原文分散的词语合并，一起译出，也是一种翻译技巧，熟练译者才会掌握。最后，"乡愁，更愁其愁"，三"愁"复用，汉语正好；对应之英文，并无重复现象，但字里行间，已有乡愁之痕迹，如 imagination has free play，想象力肆意挥洒之时，也正是乡愁酝酿之初。

望月之 136：Moonshift: the Power of the Moon（月亮的脸，偷偷地在改变）

读英文

"So you have seen my daughter?" Goriot spoke tremulously, and the sound of his voice **broke in upon Eugene's dreams**.

"这样看来，你见到我女儿了？"高老头颤颤巍巍地问道。他的声音打断了欧仁的沉思。

I always **wake up from my dreams** time to time.

我总是不时地从梦中醒来。

He sat close by a window, and his apathetic **eyes rested** now and again **on** the dreary scene without.

他靠窗边坐着，那双漠然的眼睛不时瞧着窗外凄凉的景色。

Delay **spells** danger.

延迟招致危险。

He believes **the shift in my mind** occurred when dropping prices suddenly made a big-screen TV a real possibility form.

他认为，当价格骤降让拥有一台大屏幕电视突然成为可能时，我的想法发生了改变。

She **bent her head, overcome by** a sense of unworthiness.

她难过地低下头，感到非常不值得。

英文散译

Moonshift: the Power of the Moon

A beam of silvery light breaks in upon my dream, from which I wake up, to find the bedside floor which is frostily filmy. I glance up to see a moon without the window, on which I rest my eyes. The moon spells homesickness and, there is a shift in my mind; abstractedly, I bend my head, overcome by it.

英文诗译

Moonshift: the Power of the Moon

A beam of silvery light
breaks in upon my dream,
from which I wake up,
to find the bedside floor
which is frostily filmy.
I glance up to see a moon
without the window, on
which I rest my eyes. The
moon spells homesickness
and, there is a shift in my
mind; abstractedly, I bend
my head, overcome by it.

回译

月亮的脸，偷偷地在改变
一束银光，搅扰
我的睡眠，我从
梦中醒来，发现
床前地面，如梦
似霜。抬头，只见
窗外明月——对之，
我醉心凝望。乡愁，

都是月亮惹的祸：
些许的变化，我
的所思所想；茫然
无计，我低头
沉思，沉入思乡……

译人语

英文译诗标题：*Moonshift: the Power of the Moon*，应该不太容易理解。其实，借鉴自一本英文书籍的名字：*Friendshifts: the Power of Friendship and How It Shapes Our Lives*，这本书讲友谊在我们生活当中的重要性；friendshifts 是造词，大意为"朋友的变化"。仿此，便有了《静夜思》之造词：Moonshifts；本为复数形式，但在译诗过程中，觉得采用单数更好。英文 The moon spells homesickness and, there is a shift in my mind（乡愁，都是月亮惹的祸：些许的变化，我的所思所想）：眼见明月，而内心思乡，这种心里的微妙变化，用单数 shift 即可，因此，诗题中的 Moonshifts，也由复数改成单数，以形成诗文呼应。诗题之汉语回译：《月亮的脸，偷偷地在改变》，也就有了翻译的理据；至于 the Power of the Moon，并未字面译出"月亮之魅"，但已暗含诗中之字里行间。其实，"月亮的脸，偷偷地在改变"，源自孟庭苇的歌曲《你看你看月亮的脸》，因而亲切。

月亮在中国人的生活中，扮演着重要的角色，对中国人的生活和思维模式，产生了重要的影响。中国文化，有时也叫"月亮文化"，即缘由此故。若扩而论之，写一本关于月亮在中国文化中的重要性的书，似乎可名其名：*Moonshifts: the Power of the Moon and How It Shapes the Chinese Mindset*，这里，可用复数形式的 moonshifts，暗示"月有阴晴圆缺，此事古难全。"另外，汉语回译中，"都是月亮惹的祸"，源自另一首歌曲《月亮惹的祸》，其中有一句歌词："我承认都是月亮惹的祸，那样的夜色太美你太温柔。""茫然无计"，令人想起李清照的"此情无计可消除，才下眉头却上心头"；"我低头沉思，沉入思乡……"，借助两个"沉"字，连通句脉，读之流畅。

望月之 137：Homesickness Persists in the Depth of Night （夜深乡愁生）

读英文

It seems as if everything was lighted up for me by **a ray of bright sunlight**.
这时，好像一束明亮的阳光为我点亮了一切。

The tones of her voice still **exerted a spell over him**.
她说话的语气仍然令他着迷。

This almost admiring attention **gave a new turn to his thoughts**.
这近乎钦羡的关注让他的想法有了新的转变。

Eugene, dining for the first time in a house where the traditions of grandeur had descended through many generations, had never seen any **spectacle like this that now met his eyes**.

这座府宅里有世代流传下来的高贵传统。欧仁是第一次在这样的府邸用餐，还从来没有见过眼前这般景象。

If you **look at her so persistently**, you will make people talk, M. de Rastignac.
你要是老盯着她看，就会招来别人闲话的，德拉斯蒂涅先生。

英文散译

Homesickness Persists in the Depth of Night
A ray of silvery light charms the bedside floor into a film of frost — upward

looking, the sight of a bright moon, which immediately exerts a spell over me, gives a new turn to my thoughts. In the depth of night, I am deeply touched by the spectacle like this that now meets my eyes; as I look at the moon persistently, homesickness persists.

英文诗译

Homesickness Persists in the Depth of Night

A ray of silvery light
charms the bedside
floor into a film of frost
— upward looking,
the sight of a bright
moon, which immediately
exerts a spell over me,
gives a new turn to my
thoughts. In the depth
of night, I am deeply
touched by the spectacle
like this that now meets
my eyes; as I look at
the moon persistently,
homesickness persists.

回译

夜深乡愁生
一束银光，梦
幻般，把床前
地面，敷上一层
薄薄的冷霜——
抬眼望，只见
一轮明月：立马，

令我陶醉着迷，
让我有了新的
所思、所想。
夜深，人静，
目睹着眼前这般
景象，我内心深
为感动。我恒久
盯着月亮，乡愁
袭来，怎可挡？

译人语

英义诗题 *Homesickness Persists in the Depth of Night*，与诗之结尾 homesickness persists，形成呼应；诗内，persists 与之前的 persistently，构成充分头韵，于是，英文句子: as I look at the moon persistently, homesickness persists, 余味生矣。

另外，译诗中，动词 charm 也用得较好；exerts a spell over me，gives a new turn to，the spectacle like this that now meets my eyes 等，因借鉴英文而出彩出色。其中，gives a new turn to my thoughts（让我有了新的所思、所想），与"望月之 136"中的句子: there is a shift in my mind（些许的变化，我的所思所想），有些类似，同一思路所致。汉语回译的最后，"乡愁袭来，怎可挡？"采用疑问句，英文却是陈述句；句式改变，也是翻译之常态。

望月之 138：The Sight of the Moon Fills Me with Homesickness（见月，思乡）

读英文

A ray of light pierced the darkness.

一道光线穿透黑暗。

The table **was coated in** dust.

桌子上覆盖了一层灰尘。

I feared it was coming as my boss wouldn't **meet my eye** and I knew someone had to go.

我担心事情终将发生，因为我老板不愿正视我的眼睛，而且我知道有人必须离开。

Father Goriot **watched him with eager eyes**.

高老头用渴望的眼神看着他。

He looked **meditatively** at Rastignac, and held out his hand to Maxime with a cordial "Good morning," that astonished Eugene not a little.

他把帽子留在门外，也不跟伯爵夫人打招呼，而是若有所思地看了看拉斯蒂涅，然后跟马克西姆握了握手，还热情地说了句"早上好"。这让欧仁大吃一惊。

He glanced round the squalid room, saw the eighteen poverty-stricken creatures about to feed like cattle in their stalls, and **the sight filled him with loathing**.

他环顾了一下肮脏的屋子，看到十八个穷困潦倒的家伙像马厩里的牲畜一样准备吃东西，这个场面让他非常厌恶。

What **exquisite joy** they would find in self-sacrifice!

她们从自我牺牲中得到的快乐是多么地强烈啊！

I feel exquisite pleasure in dwelling on the recollections of childhood, before misfortune had tainted my mind and changed its bright visions of extensive usefulness into gloomy and narrow reflections upon self.

我在回忆童年往事时总能感受到强烈的快乐，直到后来厄运玷污了我的思想，把我对未来的无限美好憧憬变成了阴郁、狭隘的自我反思。

英文散译

The Sight of the Moon Fills Me with Homesickness

A ray of light pierces the darkness in my room, coating the floor before my bed in silvery frost, before meeting my eye. I lift my gaze to see the moon, which I watch meditatively with eager eyes — the sight fills me with homesickness, when I feel exquisite joy and pleasure in dwelling on the recollections of childhood.

英文诗译

The Sight of the Moon Fills Me with Homesickness

A ray of light pierces
the darkness in my room,
coating the floor before
my bed in silvery frost,
before meeting my eye.
I lift my gaze to see
the moon, which I
watch meditatively
with eager eyes —
the sight fills me
with homesickness,
when I feel exquisite

joy and pleasure

in dwelling on the

recollections of childhood.

回译

见月，思乡

一道光线，穿透

屋里的黑暗，

给床前地面，

铺上一层银霜。

面对此景，我

搭眼，望见

月亮，渴望的

眼神，沉思默想

——乡愁，油然

而生：回忆着

童年往事，内心

感到无限的快乐。

译人语

英译中，the sight fills me with homesickness，呼应诗题：*The Sight of the Moon Fills Me with Homesickness*，稍有变化：题目中添加了 of the moon，以使其具体。回译汉语：《见月，思乡》，这与"望月之 139"的汉语回译高度相似：《见月思乡》。这里，只是添加了逗号，也就延缓了动作。英译中，a ray of light pierces the darkness，I watch meditatively with eager eyes，exquisite joy and pleasure 等，对"读英文"中的句子进行借鉴、改造而出，因而纯正有余味。另外，汉语回译中的"搭眼"，乃是故乡方言，大意为"放眼看去，随意看一下"。

望月之 139：The Midnight Moon as I Gaze at It（凝望：午夜之月）

读英文

Jack **woke up** the next morning **to** the sound of furniture being moved around.
次日早上，家具到处移动的声音，把杰克吵醒了。

The lawn is **carpeted with** fallen leaves.
草坪被落叶覆盖着。

At all that noise, Pinocchio **lifted his head and raised his eyes**.
听到这些声音，皮诺乔抬起头，抬眼看。

We must **trace the source of** these noxious gases.
我们必须查出毒气的来源。

The expedition **is tracing the source of** the river.
探险队正在探索河流的源头。

She gave him a quick, upward look, then **lowered her eyes**.
她飞速地抬眼看了看他，然后又垂下双眼。

He sat down again and **fell,** unconscious of his surroundings, **into deep thought**.
他再一次坐下，不顾周围的环境，陷入了沉思。

He **was consumed with curiosity**, which the sudden change in the manner of the man before him had excited to the highest pitch.

他被好奇心吞噬了。他面前这个男人的态度突然转变，让他的好奇心提高到了极点。

英文散译

The Midnight Moon as I Gaze at It

I wake up in the midnight to a silvery beam of light, which seems to carpet the floor with a thin film of frost. I lift my head and raise my eyes, to trace the source of light to the moon without the window, before lowering my eyes and falling into deep thought, consumed with homesickness.

英文诗译

The Midnight Moon as I Gaze at It

I wake up in the mid-
night to a silvery beam
of light, which seems
to carpet the floor with
a thin film of frost. I lift
my head and raise my eyes,
to trace the source of light
to the moon without the
window, before lowering
my eyes and falling into
deep thought, consumed
with homesickness.

回译

凝望：午夜之月
午夜，一束银
光，照我醒来，
似乎给床前地
面，着了一层
薄薄的冷霜。

我抬头，寻觅光
之源——见窗外
月亮；良久凝望，
然后，双目下垂，
陷入沉思，陷入
乡愁：我的家园，
我的故乡……

译人语

偶然读到一本英文书，全名是：*America Alone — the End of the World as We Know It*，汉语译文是：《美国独行——西方世界的末日》。仔细品味，感觉 as we know it，英文纯正，汉语却无法再现，译文也就舍弃了。又想起读贾平凹的散文《我读何海霞》，刘士聪英译为：He Haixia, as I Read Him，二十多年前读到如此译文，不太理解。随后，天天坚持英文阅读，终于读到类似 as I read him 的表达，终于开悟。又突然想起《静夜思》的标题英译，岂不亦可如法炮制？于是，便有了 *The Midnight Moon as I Gaze at It* 的英译。

英译中，I wake up...to，这里的介词 to，其实表示原因："因为……而醒来"，有四两拨千斤之力；随后，carpet 用作动词，较为少见，却也形象。I lift my head and raise my eyes，若无英文借鉴，读者可能会觉得重复啰嗦：既抬头，肯定抬眼，何必赘言？其实，为了描写形象：首先举头，然后凝目，也符合人之常态。汉语回译中，将两个动词分开："我抬头……凝望"，更显自然。

《静夜思》后两句中，"举头望明月"之"举头"，与"低头思故乡"之"低头"，因为只是艺术符号，很多情况下不必译出动作，译出情感即可；或者只是译出"举头"，没有译出"低头"。但在此译中，"举头"，如果说用了两个动词来译：lift 和 raise，"低头"，同样对应两个英文动词：lower 和 fall，可谓一词双译。词双而言不赘，语丰而意不重，乃汉诗英译之要旨。

望月之 140：My Heart Rings with Homesickness in the Dead of Night（半夜时分，我的心呀，充满着乡愁）

读英文

The whole city **is ringing with** his fame.

他在全市极负名望。

The whole Asia **is ringing with** his success.

整个亚洲都在传颂着他的成功。

A smile flitted over the poor girl's lips; **it seemed as if a ray of light** from her soul **had lighted up her face.**

一丝微笑掠过了这个可怜姑娘的唇边，看起来仿佛她灵魂里的一束光点亮了她的脸庞。

He drew near to the window, and placing himself so that **a ray of light should fall upon** the letter as he held it, he drew it from his pocket and read it again.

他走近窗户，站在灯光能够照到的位置，从口袋里掏出信，又看了一遍。

The innumerable thoughts that surged through his brain might be summed up in these phrases.

他脑子里涌出的无数想法可以归结为以上几句话。

As the evening of the third day came on, **his heart rang with fear.**

第三个夜晚到来时，他的心中充满了恐怖。

The land was warm with sunshine and gladness when I was a boy.
我小的时候，我们那块土地上都是暖洋洋的阳光和快乐的人们。

英文散译

My Heart Rings with Homesickness in the Dead of Night

It seems as if a cold ray of light, falling upon the bedside floor which is transformed into a thin film of frost, has lighted up my face, and there are, when I catch a glimpse of the bright moon without the window, innumerable thoughts surging through my brain. My heart rings with homesickness: I begin to miss my homeland, my dear lost land which was warm with sunshine and gladness when I was a boy.

英文诗译

My Heart Rings with Homesickness in the Dead of Night

It seems as if a cold
ray of light, falling
upon the bedside floor
which is transformed
into a thin film of frost,
has lighted up my face
in the dead of night,
and there are, when I
catch a glimpse of the
bright moon without
the window, innumerable
thoughts surging through
my brain. My heart rings
with homesickness: I begin
to miss my homeland, my
dear lost land which was
warm with sunshine and

gladness when I was a boy.

回译

半夜时分，我的心呀，充满着乡愁

一束冷光，落在

床前的地上，

朦朦胧胧地，

将其变成了一层

薄薄的银霜。

这束光，夜半时分，

点亮了我的脸庞——

当我看到窗外

之月，脑海里

涌浮出无数的思想。

我的心呀，充满着

乡愁：我开始

想念我的家乡，

我亲爱的已逝的

故乡；小时候，

那块土地上，到处

是快乐，到处是

阳光，一片暖洋洋。

译人语

英诗标题：*My Heart Rings with Homesickness in the Dead of Night*，从译诗中摘录合并而成：第七行的 in the dead of night，与第十三、十四行的 My heart rings with homesickness。其实，首先译诗，然后才考虑标题的英译问题。英文译诗中，两处用到插入成分：falling upon the bedside floor which is transformed into a thin film of frost，以及 when I catch a glimpse of the bright moon without the window，均较长，为典型的英文句法，恰符合笔者所倡导的"但为传神，不拘其形，散文笔法，诗意内容；将汉诗英译提到到英诗的高度"的译诗理念。

另外，innumerable thoughts surging through my brain，表达鲜活生动；homeland 与 land 的反复，也体现了译者的用心；my heart rings with homesickness，其中，ring with，表示"充满着，回荡着"之意，几成隽语名言，因此，从诗行中提出，作为标题；my dear lost land which was warm with sunshine and gladness when I was a boy，因有借鉴，译文向雅，对应之汉语回译："我亲爱的已逝的故乡；小时候，那块土地上，到处是快乐，到处是阳光，一片暖洋洋。"译文看似简单，其实也下了功夫："小时候"，不同于"我小的时候"，或者"在\当我小的时候"，参看《大海啊，故乡》的歌词："小时候，妈妈对我讲，大海就是我故乡"，若改动一字，效果则差矣。英文中，which，was，warm，with，when 等，构成头韵；汉语反复"到处"，并有"乡"，"上"，"光"，"洋"之韵。整首诗的汉语回译，读来颇感酣畅淋漓，因为有韵："光"，"上"，"霜"，"光"，"庞"，"想"，"乡"，"乡"，"上"，"光"，"洋"等，这些韵，或在诗行之尾，或在诗行之中，一气流壮，节奏锵然。

望月之 141：Moonlit Midnight: the Scene of My Old Home（深夜明月：老家的情景）

读英文

Gigonnet and Mitral **gave a glance at** the three clerks so penetrating, so **glittering with gleams of gold**, that the two scoffers were sobered at once.

羊腿子和米特拉尔朝那三个公务员扫了一眼。他们的眼神闪烁着金子的光芒，又如此具有穿透力，使得那两个嘲笑他们的人立刻清醒过来。

When her father died in a strange place, in a strange name, without a letter, book, or scrap of paper that yielded the faintest clue by which his friends or relatives could be **traced**—the child was taken by some wretched cottagers, who reared it as their own.

她父亲客死他乡，除了一个假名，没留下一封信、一本书，甚至是一张纸片，没法提供一星半点的线索，别人找不到他的朋友或亲戚——后来那个孩子被一户穷苦农家带走了，并将她视如己出，抚养着她。

Then he returned to her face and **looked long and intently into** her blue eyes.

接着，他又重新瞧着她的脸，长久而专注地看着她那双蓝眼睛。

A wave of yet more tender joy escaped from his heart and went coursing in warm flood along his arteries.

一股更温柔的喜悦之情从他心头溢出，在血管中欢快地奔跑着。

Mme. de Beauseant did not hear him; **she was absorbed in her own thoughts**. 德伯桑夫人没有听见他的话，她想得入神了。

As **her thoughts strayed back to the scene of** the sacrifice, and recalled the dangers which still menaced her, she shuddered with terror.

当她回想祭祀的情景，回想那些至今还对她的生命存在威胁的危险时，她就害怕得颤抖起来。

英文散译

Moonlit Midnight: the Scene of My Old Home

I give a glance at the floor glittering with gleams of frost, and the source of it is traced without the window to the midnight moon, into which I look long and intently. A wave of yet more tender joy escapes from my heart and goes coursing in warm flood along my arteries, when I am absorbed in my own thoughts, which stray back to the scene of my old home ....

英文诗译

Moonlit Midnight: the Scene of My Old Home

I give a glance at the floor
glittering with gleams of frost,
and the source of it is traced
without the window to the midnight moon, into which I look
long and intently. A wave of
yet more tender joy escapes
from my heart and goes coursing
in warm flood along my arteries,
when I am absorbed in my own
thoughts, which stray back to
the scene of my old home ....

回译

深夜明月：老家的情景
我扫一眼地面：
正闪烁着如霜
的光芒。其源：
窗外，深夜，明月
——我长久而专注
地凝视着。一股
温柔的喜悦之情，
从我心头溢出，
在血管中欢快地
奔跑着。我想得
入了神，想起
老家的情景……

译人语

英译中，I give a glance at the floor，等于 I glance at the floor，但是，含义却有微妙的流变。其间的差别，大概相当于"我扫一眼地面"与"我看地面"之间的差别。随后，with gleams of frost，直译："带着霜一样的闪烁之光"，大好；意译："正闪烁着如霜的光芒"，当然不如英文更妙。A wave of yet more tender joy，从英文借鉴而来，不用比较级亦可：A wave of yet more tender joy；但是用了，表示深夜明月温柔，而内心的喜悦之情，更加温柔。李白之《静夜思》：静夜，何所思？正是老家的情景。

望月之 142：Thoughts of Home in the Depth of Night（**深夜，想家**）

读英文

He **perceived** then, **at a glance**, that this woman was young and beautiful.
他一眼就发现那位女子年轻貌美。

The three blows were scarcely struck when the inside casement was opened, and **a light appeared through** the panes of the shutter.
刚敲过三下，里面的那层窗子就打开了，灯光从百叶窗的缝隙里透了出来。

Injun Joe lay stretched upon the ground, dead, with his face close to the crack of the door, as if **his longing eyes had been fixed**, to the latest moment, **upon** the light and the cheer of the free world outside.
印第安·乔伸着四肢躺在地上，已经死了。他的脸紧靠着门缝，好像在最后一刻，还在用企盼的眼神盯着外面自由世界里的光明和欢乐。

She emptied her mind of all **thoughts of home**.
她打消了想家的所有念头。

The leading anxiety which had hitherto absorbed every feeling being now in some measure appeased, **fancy began to wander**.
焦虑曾经占据他所有心思，此时既然已缓和了几分，他便开始幻想起来。

英文散译

Thoughts of Home in the Depth of Night

I perceive, at a glance, that a light is appearing through the window, whose shaft dreamily turns the floor into a thin film of frost. I lift my gaze at the moon, upon which my longing eyes have been fixed, and my mind is filled with thoughts of home, as my fancy begins to wander ….

英文诗译

Thoughts of Home in the Depth of Night

I perceive, at a glance,
that a light is appearing
through the window,
whose shaft dreamily
turns the floor into a thin
film of frost. I lift my
gaze at the moon, upon
which my longing eyes
have been fixed, and
my mind is filled with
thoughts of home, as my
fancy begins to wander ….

回译

深夜，想家
一眼，我就看见：
一束亮光，正从
窗户的缝隙里
透入；如梦似幻，
把床前地面变成
一层薄薄的冷霜。
抬眼，我看见

月亮，渴望的
眼神，长久地
凝望；脑子里充满
乡思，开始了
我的幻想⋯⋯

译人语

英译中，at a glance 的插入，大好：一方面，这一介词短语的表达极好；另一方面，也带来了形断意连的美学效果，可谓发挥了英文的优势。译文中的动词 appear，名词 shaft，副词 dreamily，形容词 longing，以及添加的小句 my fancy begins to wander 等，都巧妙到位，令人回味。标题的回译：《深夜，想家》，加一逗号，延缓了动作，有余味矣。"一眼"，与 at a glance，正相匹配，并与随后的"抬眼"形成呼应。最后，my fancy begins to wander，回译："开始了我的幻想"，而不是"我的幻想开始了"，更符合汉语表达之习惯。

望月之 143：Midnight Moon: Home Thoughts Gathering in My Heart （深夜之月：内心乡思）

读英文

The tide was going out, and the sand was smooth and **glittering**.
潮水正在退去，沙滩平坦，闪闪发亮。

My clothes can **transform** into lots of styles.
我设计的衣服，可以转变成许多风格。

He would **steal upward glances at** the clock.
他不时偷偷往上看钟。

Casting glances here and there, he seemed to be looking for somebody.
他左顾右盼，像是在找人。

He saw faint rose tints through the cashmere of the dressing gown; it had fallen slightly open, giving glimpses of a bare throat, **on which the student's eyes rested**.
　　他透过山羊绒睡裙看到了她浅粉色的肌肤。通过微微散开的睡裙，他可以时不时地瞥见她光洁的脖子。这个学生就死死盯在那里。

Eugene sat **absorbed in thought for a few moments before** plunging into his law books.
　　欧仁在全身心读法律书之前，先坐在那里出神地想了一会儿。

As **his fancy wandered** among these lofty regions in the great world of Paris,

innumerable dark **thoughts gathered in his heart**; his ideas widened, and his conscience grew more elastic.

他的幻想游走在巴黎这个宏大世界的上流社会，脑子里聚集了无数坏念头，他的眼界更宽了，良知也变得更加能屈能伸了。

英文散译

Midnight Moon: Home Thoughts Gathering in My Heart

A glittering beam of light, seeping through the window, seems to transform the floor before my bed into a thin film of frost — casting upward glances at the moon, on which my eyes rest, I am absorbed in thought for a few moments, before my fancy wanders away, with innumerable home thoughts gathering in my heart....

英文诗译

Midnight Moon: Home Thoughts Gathering in My Heart

A glittering beam of light,
seeping through the window,
seems to transform the floor
before my bed into a thin
film of frost — casting
upward glances at the moon,
on which my eyes rest, I
am absorbed in thought for
a few moments, before my
fancy wanders away, with
innumerable home thoughts
gathering in my heart....

回译

深夜之月：内心乡思
一束闪烁之光，
从窗户渗入，似乎
把我床前的地面，

变成了一层薄薄
的冷霜——抬望眼，
一轮月亮，我的
眼睛盯着不放；
半晌，我出神地
想啊想。然后，我
收拢了幻想；而无数
想家的念头啊，正
聚集着，在我的心上。

译人语

英文诗题 *Midnight Moon: Home Thoughts Gathering in My Heart*，回译《深夜之月：内心乡思》，英文单词 Gathering 的动态含义，就流失殆尽了。翻译，总是无可奈何花落去。因此，译者当发挥译文之优势，才能凑效。汉语回译中，使用"抬望眼"、"一轮月亮"、"盯着不放"、"半晌"、"收拢"等地道之汉语词汇，取得大体相当之诗性效果。总体观之，英文译诗一气呵成；汉语回译也竭力模仿，特别是通过使用分号，达到了一定的效果。

望月之 144：In the Depth of Night, My Native Land in My Thoughts（深夜时分，心念故乡）

读英文

The sun's rays, peeping at dawn **through** the trees, by-and-by to be obscured behind gathering clouds, leaving naught but gloom around, **give to** this spot the alternations of morning and night.

若夫日出而林霏开，云归而岩穴暝，晦明变化者，山间之朝暮也。

The district of Ch'u is entirely surrounded by hills, and the peaks to the south-west are clothed with a dense and beautiful growth of trees, over which **the eye wanders in raptures away to** the confines of Shantung.

环滁皆山也。其西南诸峰，林壑尤美。

The man, **lost in memories of a time long gone**, asked.

回忆着久远的过去，那人问道。

Those days might, without exaggeration, be called spacious days: and if they are gone beyond recall let us hope, at least, that in gatherings such as this we shall still speak of them with pride and affection, **still cherish in our hearts the memory of** those dead and gone great ones whose fame the world will not willingly let die.

那些年代，毫不夸张地说，可以被称为是自由的年代：如果它们超越了记忆，那就让我们祈愿，至少，在像这样的聚会中，我们将会依旧满怀自豪和情感地谈论起它们，依旧在我们的心里珍藏对那些逝去之人的回忆，这个世界将永不会让他们的声名消亡。

I had them still in my thoughts.
我还惦记着他们。

英文散译

In the Depth of Night, My Native Land in My Thoughts

The moon's rays, peeping in the depth of night through the window, give to the room a dreamy scene where the floor seems to be frostily filmed. My eyes wander, in raptures, away from the floor to the moon without the window, and I am lost in memories of a time long gone, which are still cherished in my heart. I have my native land in my thoughts.

英文诗译

In the Depth of Night, My Native Land in My Thoughts

The moon's rays, peeping
in the depth of night through
the window, give to the room
a dreamy scene where the floor
seems to be frostily filmed.
My eyes wander, in raptures,
away from the floor to the moon
without the window, and I am
lost in memories of a time
long gone, which are still
cherished in my heart. I have
my native land in my thoughts.

回译

深夜时分，心念故乡
月亮之光，深夜，
窥视入窗，给房间

里带来梦幻的景象：
地面似乎敷了一层
薄薄的冷霜。如醉
如痴，我的目光
离开地面，看向
窗外的月亮——
回忆着久远的过去，
我内心的珍藏；
一直惦记着啊
——我的故乡。

译人语

英译中，The moon's rays give to the room a dreamy scene…，如此表达，很好；中间却又插入一个短语：peeping in the depth of night through the window，一方面拟人，一方面调节了语气和节奏，带来很好的语言审美效果。随后，再次使用插入短语 in raptures，形断意连的效果，得以加强。最后一个短句：I have my native land in my thoughts，突出强调了思乡之情。

另外，"读英文"中前两个句子，为欧阳修《醉翁亭记》之英译，译者是英国著名汉学家 Herbert A. Giles。好的译文，可以当原文来读；可惜，达到这一翻译水平的译作，并不多见。想起中学语文课本中高尔基的散文《海燕》，译文真是地道，跟中国作家写出的散文，语言上没有丝毫的逊色。Herbert A. Giles 英译的《醉翁亭记》，同样，跟英美作家笔下的散文，在语言上也不差分毫。这，才是译者应当追求的水平和境界。

望月之 145：A Longing to Be Home in the Dead of Night（深夜，渴望回家）

读英文

I crept out of bed **in the dead of night** and sneaked downstairs.
深夜我悄悄地从床上爬起来，蹑手蹑脚地下了楼。

They drained the swamp and **turned it into** fertile land.
他们排去沼泽地的水，将它变成了肥沃的土地。

The certainty of success is **a source of** happiness to which men do not confess, and all the charm of certain women lies in this.
男人的幸福感源于对成功的把握。对此，男人并不承认，但有些女人认定这是他们的魅力所在。

There is **dead silence** in the castle.
古堡内死一般的沉寂。

There was a moment of **dead silence**.
一时鸦雀无声。

A longing to wring his neck **comes over me** now and then.
我有时渴望能扭断他的脖子。

英文散译

A Longing to Be Home in the Dead of Night
A beam of light, glittering through the window, turns the floor into an icy film

of frost, the source of which is traced to a bright moon in the high night sky, the sole thing alive in the dead silence of the nature. A longing to be home, all of a sudden, comes over me.

英文诗译

A Longing to Be Home in the Dead of Night
A beam of light,
glittering through the
window, turns the floor
into an icy film of frost,
the source of which is
traced to a bright moon
in the high night sky,
the sole thing alive
in the dead silence
of the nature. A longing
to be home, all of a
sudden, comes over me.

回译

深夜，渴望回家
一束光，闪烁，
透窗，敷地面
一层薄薄的冰冷
之霜。求其源——
一轮明月，悬于
高高的夜空之中，
一片清朗。万籁
俱寂，月亮发出
唯一的声响。
渴望回家，渴望，

突然，我有了
回家的渴望。

译人语

诗题中，汉语的"渴望"，为平淡之词；英文的 longing，却耐人寻味。英文 in the Dead of Night，有"死寂"之字眼，汉语"深夜"，却无此联想。因此，英文诗题 *A Longing to Be Home in the Dead of Night*，比之汉语回译《深夜，渴望回家》，显然更有余味。整体观之，英诗通过分词短语、名词短语、从句、插入成分等，造成了英文的繁缛盘缠，如枝如蔓——由一个长句和一个短句构成。汉语回译通过逗号、内韵（光、窗、霜、朗、响、望）和反复等手段，用四个小句译出，符合汉语语言的行文特征。

望月之 146：A Moonlit Night: My Native Land Out of Sight, Never Out of Mind（月照之夜：故乡，从未断了念想）

读英文

We saw **a spark of light** through the trees.
我们透过树丛看到闪光。

Several times an hour **a spark of light** will **gradually grow into** a burning flame **that lights up** the entire building.
从一小时几次迸发的光线逐渐增长为一团燃烧的火焰，点亮了整个建筑。

To **translate** ideas **into** action.
使思想变为行动。

Imber had crossed the street and was standing there, a gaunt and hungry-looking shadow, **his gaze riveted upon** the girl.
英勃尔已经穿过马路，站在那里，他身形消瘦，面带饥容，像一个影子，他的眼睛一动不动地盯着埃米丽。

On the way thither he **indulged in the wild intoxicating dreams which fill a young head so full of delicious excitement**.
一路上，他都沉浸于狂野而醉人的幻想中。这些幻想填满了年轻人本来就满是激动之情的脑海。

How they long to **get a sight of** their **native land**!

他们多么渴望看一看故乡啊！

Out of sight, out of mind.

眼不见，心不烦。

英文散译

A Moonlit Night: My Native Land Out of Sight, Never Out of Mind

I seem to see a little spark of light seeping through the window, which gradually grows into an illuminant that lights up the room, translating the floor into an ethereal film of frost. Slowly I lift up my gaze, which rivets upon the bright moon without the window, and I begin to indulge in the wild intoxicating dreams which fill my head so full of delicious excitement — dreams about my native land which, out of sight for dozens of years, is never out of mind.

英文诗译

A Moonlit Night: My Native Land Out of Sight, Never Out of Mind

I seem to see a little spark
of light seeping through the
window, which gradually grows
into an illuminant that lights
up the room, translating the
floor into an ethereal film
of frost. Slowly I lift up my
gaze, which rivets upon the
bright moon without the window,
and I begin to indulge in the
wild intoxicating dreams
which fill my head so full
of delicious excitement —
dreams about my native land
which, out of sight for dozens
of years, is never out of mind.

回译

月照之夜：故乡，从未断了念想

我似乎看见，窗户上，

有些微的闪光，渗入，

慢慢聚光，把屋子

照亮；地面，随之

敷上了一层，若有

似无的薄霜。慢慢地，

我抬起目光，定格

在窗外的月亮之上

——开始沉浸在狂野

而醉人的幻想。这些

幻想，填满了我本就

满是激动之情的脑海

——填满了梦想，

梦想着我的故乡：

虽数十年不见，

却从未断了念想。

译人语

英文成语：Out of sight, out of mind（眼不见，心不烦），英译变其意而用
之：*A Moonlit Night: My Native Land Out of Sight, Never Out of Mind*，回译汉语：
《月照之夜：故乡，从未断了念想》，少了英文复用 out of 之妙，用"断了念
想"的地道汉语出之，亦可。英译中，illuminant，词典释意为"光源；发光体"，
但汉语回译却不能如此直译，变成了动词："把屋子照亮"。英文擅用名词，汉
语却不如此；如英文之 -er 后缀类词，译成汉语时，常用动词，便是典型之例。
英译中，随后的动词 translate，非是"翻译"，乃是"使转变；使变化"之意。
译文最后，out of sight for dozens of years, is never out of mind（虽数十年不见，
却从未断了念想），与诗题呼应。

望月之 147：The Moon Holds Me Spellbound in the Still Night（静夜之月，迷人）

读英文

The house was still except for the faint, gasping cough of his old father, whose room was opposite to his own across the middle room.

房子里静悄悄的，只有他年迈的父亲的微弱咳嗽声。他父亲的房间在堂屋的另一头，与他的房间对着。

The rain spat **icily** down and we all felt rather chilly.

雨冰冷地哗啦哗啦地下着，我们都觉得冷飕飕的。

She is the prettiest, most **ethereal** romantic heroine in the movies.

她是那些电影中最美丽、最优雅浪漫的女主角。

This meant of course that Doris had to tell Bass whether it was **a flashing light** or whether it was a steady light.

当然，这意味着桃瑞丝必须告诉巴斯这是一盏闪烁的灯，还是一盏稳定的灯。

"Who is G. C.?" answered Miss Ivors, **turning her eyes upon** him.

"谁是 G. C.？"艾弗斯小姐应答道，眼睛注视着他。

The show **held us spellbound**.

表演使我们看得入了迷。

I threw myself into the chaise that was to convey me away and **indulged in the most melancholy reflections**.

我钻进将载我远行的马车，陷入最伤感的沉思当中。

英文散译

The Moon Holds Me Spellbound in the Still Night

The room is still except for a ray of light glittering through the window — as I wake up from my dream I come to see it, before finding the floor icily coated with an ethereal film of frost. I trace the source of flashing light to the spellbinding moon in the night sky, upon which I turn my eyes. The moon holds me spellbound, and I begin to be homesick, indulging in the most melancholy reflections.

英文诗译

The Moon Holds Me Spellbound in the Still Night

The room is still except
for a ray of light glittering
through the window —
as I wake up from my dream
I come to see it, before
finding the floor icily coated
with an ethereal film of frost.
I trace the source of flashing
light to the spellbinding
moon in the night sky, upon
which I turn my eyes.
The moon holds me spell-
bound, and I begin to be
homesick, indulging in the
most melancholy reflections.

回译

静夜之月，迷人
房间里静悄悄的，
除了一束光线，
闪闪烁烁，透窗
而入——当我
从梦中醒来，我
看见这幅景象。
然后，发现地面
冰冷，梦幻如霜。
追光求源，只见
夜空之中，一轮
迷人的月亮，我
眼睛盯着不放。
月亮迷我，我开始
想家，陷入乡思
之中，满怀着感伤。

译人语

英译中，as I wake up from my dream I come to see it，看似简单，其实模仿地道之英文而来。望月之 122 的英译，striving to construct a mental picture of the home as I have seen it in my childhood，以及望月之 139 诗题的英译：*The Midnight Moon as I Gaze at It*，已有类似之运用。回顾英文书名：*America Alone — the End of the World as We Know It*，及其汉译：《美国独行——西方世界的末日》。再回顾刘士聪对于贾平凹散文《我读何海霞》的标题英译：*He Haixia, as I Read Him*，便觉英文表达之微妙。比读英汉之间：as I wake up from my dream I come to see it，所对应的汉语回译："当我从梦中醒来，我看见这幅景象"，显然平淡了许多。

望月之 148: A Bright Moon Brings Me Homeward (明月照我把家还)

读英文

The light glowed through the kitchen windows onto the floors of the old farmhouse where I stood waiting.

光线透过厨房窗户，照在这古老农舍地面上，我就站在这里等着。

I have been at his **bedside** since he became ill.

自从他生病以来，我一直在他的床边陪伴着他。

A thin film formed on the surface of the pulp.

纸浆表面结了一层膜。

As the bell chimed, Helen took my small hand and **turned it upward** in hers.

铃响了，海伦抓住我的小手，朝上，放进她的手掌里。

Then they waited in silence for what seemed a long time. The hooting of a distant owl was all the sound that troubled **the dead stillness**.

他们静静地等了似乎很长一段时间，除了远处猫头鹰的叫声外，周围是一片死寂。

By the time **the moon was high**, they carried their bounty of apple-lumped bags to the jeep and placed them around my sleeping body.

月亮高悬空中之时，他们扛着赏赐得来的鼓鼓囊囊的几袋苹果，来到吉普车旁，放在我的身边，我正熟睡着。

英文散译

A Bright Moon Brings Me Homeward

A shaft of light glows through the window onto the bedside floor, which seems to be turned into a thin film of frost. I turn my eyes upward, to find, through the dead stillness of air, a bright moon which is high in the sky, and I am transported far away, to my long lost hometown.

英文诗译

A Bright Moon Brings Me Homeward

A shaft of light glows
through the window
onto the bedside floor,
which seems to be
turned into a thin film
of frost. I turn my eyes
upward, to find, through
the dead stillness of air,
a bright moon which is
high in the sky, and I am
transported far away, to
my long lost hometown.

回译

明月照我把家还
一束光，亮透
窗户，落在
床前的地上，
地面随之幻成
一层薄薄的白
霜。抬眼远望，
透过死寂的

空气，我看见
一轮月亮，高悬
空中——我神游
远方，回到阔
别已久的故乡。

译人语

英文诗题：*A Bright Moon Brings Me Homeward*，自然，而好；汉语回译：《明月照我把家还》，有民歌之风味。译诗开头：A shaft of light glows through the window onto the bedside floor，其中介词：through 与 onto，有明显的动词意味。随后，turned 和 turn，虽然重复动词，含义却有流变：前者为"变成"，后者为"看向"，有同源词语之修辞意味。介词短语 through the dead stillness of air（透过死寂的空气）——如此望月，具有新诗之意味。想起李白《玉阶怨》中后两句："却卜水晶帘，玲珑望秋月"，以及庞德的英译：I let down the crystal curtain, \ and watch the moon through the clear autumn，介词 through 的使用，具同一旨趣。

望月之 149：Homesickness Is Stirred in the Moonlit Night（月照之夜，乡愁涌动）

读英文

She **had given her face a dab with** a wet towel.
她用湿毛巾把脸略略擦了一下。

Join love thereto, the warmth of gratitude that all generous souls feel for **the source of their pleasures**, and you have the explanation of many strange incongruities in human nature.
爱情是慷慨之人的快乐之源，让他们心怀感激，无比温暖。将保护欲和爱情放在一起，你就能解释人性中很多奇特的不协调现象。

Cut me just **a small sliver of** cheese.
给我切一小片干酪吧。

I imagined only mist over the pond, **a sliver of moon** in a dark sky, scatterings of stars, birdsong.
我想象着，池塘上的迷雾，黯淡的空中，露出一小片月亮，稀稀落落的星星，以及鸟叫声。

Blood was beginning to **seep through** the bandages.
血开始从绷带上渗出来。

Whereupon this insolent being, who, doubtless, had a right to be insolent, sang an Italian trill, and went towards the window where Eugene was standing, moved thereto quite as much by a desire to see the student's face as by a wish to **look out into the courtyard**.

毋庸置疑，这个傲慢的男人有他傲慢的资本。他说话时带着意大利语的颤音，朝欧仁站着的窗户边走来。他既想看看这个法律系学生的脸，也想看窗外的院子。

A sensation of tenderness filled the air.
空气中充满了温存的情感气息。

He was still under the spell of youthful beliefs, he had just left home, pure and sacred **feelings had been stirred within him**, and this was his first day on the battlefield of civilization in Paris.

他的心里仍保存着年轻人的信仰。他刚离家不久，心里还装着纯洁、高尚的亲情，这还是他在巴黎初次体验文明的战场。

He had relapsed into the **dreamy state of mind** that these superficial observers took for senile torpor, due to his lack of intelligence.

他重新恢复了迷迷糊糊的思想状态。这些肤浅的观察者把那种状态看成是老年人迟钝的表现，因为他太傻了。

Visions rose before his eyes.
他的眼前浮现出一幅幅画面。

英文散译

Homesickness Is Stirred in the Moonlit Night

A dab seems to be given to my bedside floor with a fine powder of frost, the source of which is traced to a small sliver of moonlight seeping through the window. Looking out into the courtyard silently bathed in the watery moonlight, I feel a sensation of tenderness filling the night air — homesickness is stirred within me and, in a dreamy state of mind, domestic visions begin to rise before my eyes.

英文诗译

Homesickness Is Stirred in the Moonlit Night

A dab seems to be given

to my bedside floor
with a fine powder
of frost, the source
of which is traced to
a small sliver of moon-
light seeping through
the window. Looking
out into the courtyard
silently bathed in the
watery moonlight, I feel
a sensation of tenderness
filling the night air —
homesickness is stirred
within me and, in a
dreamy state of mind,
domestic visions begin
to rise before my eyes.

回译

月照之夜，乡愁涌动
床前地上，似乎
轻轻敷上了一层
白白的薄霜。
追光求源——
一小片月光，
正从窗户的
缝隙里渗透
而入。看向
院子：静谧；
如水的月光，
我感到一股股

柔情，正充溢

着夜晚的空气

——乡愁涌动；

我心，如入梦乡；

眼前，浮现出

一幅幅画面，

都是亲切的故乡！

译人语

英译 A dab seems to be given to my bedside floor with a fine powder of frost，借鉴自英文句子：She had given her face a dab with a wet towel.（她用湿毛巾把脸略略擦了一下。）由主动语态到被动语态，语气更加委婉细腻。随后，a small sliver of moonlight（一小片月光）中，名词 sliver，为"裂片；细长条"之意，颇具诗意。I feel a sensation of tenderness filling the night air（我感到一股股柔情，正充溢着夜晚的空气），写见月光，而内心充满柔情；此情，由心而向外，注情于物。最后，domestic visions begin to rise before my eyes，描写形象，栩栩如生；汉语回译："眼前，浮现出一幅幅画面，都是亲切的故乡！"稍有变通。

望月之 150：Moon-scape & Moon-gazing（月景 · 月观）

读英文

Those are days when **the whole world shines radiant with light**, when everything glows and sparkles before the eyes of youth, days that bring joyous energy that is never brought into harness, days of debts and of painful fears that go hand in hand with every delight.

那些日子里，整个世界都光芒四射，一切都在年轻人眼里熠熠生辉；那些日子里，他充满了根本无法控制的快乐能量；那些日子里，负罪感和痛苦的恐惧感与一切愉悦感并存。

The moonlight lit the snowy clearing with **a pale luminescence**.
月亮用其淡淡的冷光，照亮了积雪的空地。

The man **glanced from the lady's face to** the little egg-shaped head and back again; and, almost before he was aware of it, his tongue had found a felicitous moment.

男人把目光从这位女士的脸上转到了那个鸡蛋一样的脑袋上，他的舌头下意识地抓住了这个时机。

The man said approvingly, **his eyes passing tenderly over the girl** as she swung the horse around.

男人赞许地说着，当女孩扬鞭策马时，他的眼睛充满柔情地向女孩望去。

…a yellow orb of moon hanging in the darkening sky out the window.

一个黄色的月球，悬挂在窗外黯淡的空中。

The blood went bounding along his veins; and the **thoughts went rioting through his brain,** proud, joyful, tender, valorous.

血液在他的血管里跳跃，各种念头在他脑子里骚动不安：骄傲，欢乐，温柔以及勇敢。

Grubless, spiritless, **with a lust for home in their hearts,** they had been staked by the P. C. Company to cut wood for its steamers, with the promise at the end of a passage home.

他们饥肠辘辘，无精打采，非常想回家。他们受到 P.C.公司的资助，为它的汽船伐木，公司承诺最后会给他们回家的路费。

英文散译

Moon-scape & Moon-gazing

The room shines with a dim light, which transforms the floor into a pale luminescence, like a thin film of frost. I glance up from the floor to the window, my eyes passing tenderly over a brilliant orb of moon hanging in the boundless sky out the window, when thoughts go rioting through my brain, with a lust for home in my heart.

英文诗译

Moon-scape & Moon-gazing

The room shines with
a dim light, which
transforms the floor
into a pale luminescence,
like a thin film of frost.
I glance up from the floor
to the window, my eyes
passing tenderly over
a brilliant orb of moon

hanging in the boundless
sky out the window,
when thoughts go rioting
through my brain, with a
lust for home in my heart.

回译

月景 · 月观
屋里，微微发亮，
地面幻成淡淡
的冷光，好像
一层薄薄的冷霜。
目光从地面，
看向门窗——
充满柔情，看着
灿烂的月球，
悬挂在窗外
无边的空中；
各种念头，在我
脑子里，不安，
骚动；心里有着
对家乡的思念。

译人语

英诗标题 Moon-scape & Moon-gazing，重复 moon，并利用复合词，形成两个单词之间的平行或对称，效果较好。汉语回译:《月景 · 月观》，如法炮制，具同一效果。译文中，which transforms the floor into a pale luminescence（地面幻成淡淡的冷光），描写生动细腻；my eyes passing tenderly over a brilliant orb of moon hanging in the boundless sky out the window, when thoughts go rioting through my brain, with a lust for home in my heart（充满柔情，看着灿烂的月球，悬挂在窗外无边的空中；各种念头，在我脑子里，不安，骚动；心里有着对家

乡的思念），因为借鉴，译文终于算得上一流的文学作品。由此看来，汉诗英译中的"拿来主义"，值得提倡和发扬光大。